I Will Repay

Baroness Emmuska Orczy

I Will Repay

The present edition is a reproduction of previous publication of this classic work. Minor typographical errors may have been corrected without note, however, for an authentic reading experience the spelling, punctuation, and capitalization have been retained from the original text.

ISBN: 978-1-64799-111-1

CONTENTS

PROLOGUE

I

Paris: 1783

"Coward! Coward! Coward!"

The words rang out, clear, strident, passionate, in a crescendo of agonised humiliation.

The boy, quivering with rage, had sprung to his feet, and, losing his balance, he fell forward clutching at the table, whilst with a convulsive movement of the lids, he tried in vain to suppress the tears of shame which were blinding him.

"Coward!" He tried to shout the insult so that all might hear, but his parched throat refused him service, his trembling hand sought the scattered cards upon the table, he collected them together, quickly, nervously, fingering them with feverish energy, then he hurled them at the man opposite, whilst with a final effort he still contrived to mutter: "Coward!"

The older men tried to interpose, but the young ones only laughed, quite prepared for the adventure which must inevitably ensue, the only possible ending to a quarrel such as this.

Conciliation or arbitration was out of the question. Déroulède should have known better than to speak disrespectfully of Adèle de Montchéri, when the little Vicomte de Marny's infatuation for the notorious beauty had been the talk of Paris and Versailles these many months past.

Adèle was very lovely and a veritable tower of greed and egotism. The Marnys were rich and the little Vicomte very young, and just now the brightly-plumaged hawk was busy plucking the latest pigeon, newly arrived from its ancestral cote.

The boy was still in the initial stage of his infatuation. To him Adèle was a paragon of all the virtues, and he would have done battle on her behalf against the entire aristocracy of France, in a vain endeavour to justify his own exalted opinion of one of the most dissolute women of the epoch. He was a first-rate swordsman too, and his friends had already learned that it was best to avoid all allusions to Adèle's beauty and weaknesses.

But Déroulède was a noted blunderer. He was little versed in the manners and tones of that high society in which, somehow, he still seemed an intruder. But for his great wealth, no doubt, he never would have been admitted within the intimate circle of aristocratic France. His ancestry was somewhat doubtful and his coat-of-arms unadorned with quarterings.

But little was known of his family or the origin of its wealth; it was only known that his father had suddenly become the late King's dearest friend, and commonly surmised that Déroulède gold had on more than one occasion filled the emptied coffers of the First Gentleman of France.

Déroulède had not sought the present quarrel. He had merely blundered in that clumsy way of his, which was no doubt a part of the inheritance bequeathed to him by his bourgeois ancestry.

He knew nothing of the little Vicomte's private affairs, still less of his relationship with Adèle, but he knew enough of the world and enough of Paris to be acquainted with the lady's reputation. He hated at all times to speak of women. He was not what in those days would be termed a ladies' man, and was even somewhat unpopular with the sex. But in this instance the conversation had drifted in that direction, and when Adèle's name was mentioned, every one became silent, save the little Vicomte, who waxed enthusiastic.

A shrug of the shoulders on Déroulède's part had aroused the boy's ire, then a few casual words, and, without further warning, the insult had been hurled and the cards thrown in the older man's face.

Déroulède did not move from his seat. He sat erect and placid, one knee crossed over the other, his serious, rather swarthy face perhaps a shade paler than usual: otherwise it seemed as if the insult had never reached his ears, or the cards struck his cheek.

He had perceived his blunder, just twenty seconds too late. Now he was sorry for the boy and angered with himself, but it was too late to draw back. To avoid a conflict he would at this moment have sacrificed half his fortune, but not one particle of his dignity.

He knew and respected the old Duc de Marny, a feeble old man now, almost a dotard whose hitherto spotless blason , the young Vicomte, his son, was doing his best to besmirch.

When the boy fell forward, blind and drunk with rage, Déroulède leant towards him automatically, quite kindly, and helped him to his feet. He would have asked the lad's pardon for his own thoughtlessness, had that been possible: but the stilted code of so-called honour forbade so logical a proceeding. It would have done no good, and could but imperil his own reputation without averting the traditional sequel.

The panelled walls of the celebrated gaming saloon had often witnessed scenes such as this. All those present acted by routine. The etiquette of duelling prescribed certain formalities, and these were strictly but rapidly adhered to.

v

The young Vicomte was quickly surrounded by a close circle of friends. His great name, his wealth, his father's influence, had opened for him every door in Versailles and Paris. At this moment he might have had an army of seconds to support him in the coming conflict.

Déroulède for a while was left alone near the card table, where the unsnuffed candles began smouldering in their sockets. He had risen to his feet, somewhat bewildered at the rapid turn of events. His dark, restless eyes wandered for a moment round the room, as if in quick search for a friend.

But where the Vicomte was at home by right, Déroulède had only been admitted by reason of his wealth. His acquaintances and sycophants were many, but his friends very few.

For the first time this fact was brought home to him. Every one in the room must have known and realised that he had not wilfully sought this quarrel, that throughout he had borne himself as any gentleman would, yet now, when the issue was so close at hand, no one came forward to stand by him.

"For form's sake, monsieur, will you choose your seconds?"

It was the young Marquis de Villefranche who spoke, a little haughtily, with a certain ironical condescension towards the rich parvenu, who was about to have the honour of crossing swords with one of the noblest gentlemen in France.

"I pray you, Monsieur le Marquis," rejoined Déroulède coldly, "to make the choice for me. You see, I have few friends in Paris."

The Marquis bowed, and gracefully flourished his lace handkerchief. He was accustomed to being appealed to in all matters pertaining to etiquette, to the toilet, to the latest cut in coats, and the procedure in duels. Good-natured, foppish, and idle, he felt quite happy and in his element thus to be made chief organiser of the tragic farce, about to be enacted on the parquet floor of the gaming saloon.

He looked about the room for a while, scrutinising the faces of those around him. The gilded youth was crowding round De Marny; a few older men stood in a group at the farther end of the room: to these the Marquis turned, and addressing one of them, an elderly man with a military bearing and a shabby brown coat:

"Mon Colonel," he said, with another flourishing bow; "I am deputed by M. Déroulède to provide him with seconds for this affair of honour, may I call upon you to ..."

"Certainly, certainly," replied the Colonel. "I am not intimately acquainted with M. Déroulède, but since you stand sponsor, M. le Marquis ..."

"Oh!" rejoined the Marquis, lightly, "a mere matter of form, you know. M. Déroulède belongs to the entourage of Her Majesty. He is a man of honour. But I am not his sponsor. Marny is my friend, and if you prefer not to ..."

"Indeed I am entirely at M. Déroulède's service," said the Colonel, who had thrown a quick, scrutinising glance at the isolated figure near the card table, "if he will accept my services ..."

"He will be very glad to accept, my dear Colonel," whispered the Marquis with an ironical twist of his aristocratic lips. "He has no friends in our set, and if you and De Quettare will honour him, I think he should be grateful."

M. de Quettare, adjutant to M. le Colonel, was ready to follow in the footsteps of his chief, and the two men, after the prescribed salutations to M. le Marquis de Villefranche, went across to speak to Déroulède.

"If you will accept our services, monsieur," began the Colonel abruptly, "mine, and my adjutant's, M. de Quettare, we place ourselves entirely at your disposal."

"I thank you, messieurs," rejoined Déroulède. "The whole thing is a farce, and that young man is a fool; but I have been in the wrong and ..."

"You would wish to apologise?" queried the Colonel icily.

The worthy soldier had heard something of Déroulède's reputed bourgeois ancestry. This suggestion of an apology was no doubt in accordance with the customs of the middle-classes, but the Colonel literally gasped at the unworthiness of the proceeding. An apology? Bah! Disgusting! cowardly! beneath the dignity of any gentleman, however wrong he might be. How could two soldiers of His Majesty's army identify themselves with such doings?

But Déroulède seemed unconscious of the enormity of his suggestion.

"If I could avoid a conflict," he said, "I would tell the Vicomte that I had no knowledge of his admiration for the lady we were discussing and ..."

"Are you so very much afraid of getting a sword scratch, monsieur?" interrupted the Colonel impatiently, whilst M. de Quettare elevated a pair of aristocratic eyebrows in bewilderment at such an extraordinary display of bourgeois cowardice.

"You mean, Monsieur le Colonel?"—queried Déroulède.

"That you must either fight the Vicomte de Marny to-night, or clear out of Paris to-morrow. Your position in our set would become untenable," retorted the Colonel, not unkindly, for in spite of Déroulède's extraordinary attitude, there was nothing in his bearing or his appearance that suggested cowardice or fear.

"I bow to your superior knowledge of your friends, M. le Colonel," responded Déroulède, as he silently drew his sword from its sheath.

The centre of the saloon was quickly cleared. The seconds measured the length of the swords and then stood behind the antagonists, slightly in advance of the groups of spectators, who stood massed all round the room.

They represented the flower of what France had of the best and noblest in name, in lineage, in chivalry, in that year of grace 1783. The storm-cloud which a few years hence was destined to break over their heads, sweeping them from their palaces to the prison and the guillotine, was only gathering very slowly in the dim horizon of squalid, starving Paris: for the next half-dozen years they would still dance and gamble, fight and flirt, surround a tottering throne, and hoodwink a weak monarch. The Fates' avenging sword still rested in its sheath; the relentless, ceaseless wheel still bore them up in their whirl of pleasure; the downward movement had only just begun: the cry of the oppressed children of France had not yet been heard above the din of dance music and lovers' serenades.

The young Duc de Châteaudun was there, he who, nine years later, went to the guillotine on that cold September morning, his hair dressed in the latest fashion, the finest Mechlin lace around his wrists, playing a final game of piquet with his younger brother, as the tumbril bore them along through the hooting, yelling crowd of the half-naked starvelings of Paris.

There was the Vicomte de Mirepoix, who, a few years later, standing on the platform of the guillotine, laid a bet with M. de Miranges that his own blood would flow bluer than that of any other head cut off that day in France. Citizen Samson heard the bet made, and when De Mirepoix's head fell into the basket, the headsman lifted it up for M. de Miranges to see. The latter laughed.

"Mirepoix was always a braggart," he said lightly, as he laid his head upon the block.

"Who'll take my bet that my blood turns out to be bluer than his?"

But of all these comedies, these tragico-farces of later years, none who were present on that night, when the Vicomte de Marny fought Paul Déroulède, had as yet any presentiment.

They watched the two men fighting, with the same casual interest, at first, which they would have bestowed on the dancing of a new movement in the minuet.

De Marny came of a race that had wielded the sword of many centuries, but he was hot, excited, not a little addled with wine and rage. Déroulède was lucky; he would come out of the affair with a slight scratch.

A good swordsman too, that wealthy parvenu. It was interesting to watch his sword-play: very quiet at first, no feint or parry, scarcely a riposte, only en garde, always en garde very carefully, steadily, ready for his antagonist at every turn and in every circumstance.

Gradually the circle round the combatants narrowed. A few discreet exclamations of admiration greeted Déroulède's most successful parry. De Marny was getting more and more excited, the older man more and more sober and reserved.

A thoughtless lunge placed the little Vicomte at his opponent's mercy. The next instant he was disarmed, and the seconds were pressing forward to end the conflict.

Honour was satisfied: the parvenu and the scion of the ancient race had crossed swords over the reputation of one of the most dissolute women in France. Déroulède's moderation was a lesson to all the hot-headed young bloods who toyed with their lives, their honour, their reputation as lightly as they did with their lace-edged handkerchiefs and gold snuff-boxes.

Already Déroulède had drawn back. With the gentle tact peculiar to kindly people, he avoided looking at his disarmed antagonist. But something in the older man's attitude seemed to further nettle the over-stimulated sensibility of the young Vicomte.

"This is no child's play, monsieur," he said excitedly. "I demand full satisfaction."

"And are you not satisfied?" queried Déroulède. "You have borne yourself bravely, you have fought in honour of your liege lady. I, on the other hand ..."

"You," shouted the boy hoarsely, "you shall publicly apologise to a noble and virtuous woman whom you have outraged—now—at—once—on your knees ..."

"You are mad, Vicomte," rejoined Déroulède coldly. "I am willing to ask your forgiveness for my blunder ..."

"An apology—in public—on your knees ..."

The boy had become more and more excited. He had suffered humiliation after humiliation. He was a mere lad, spoilt, adulated, pampered from his boyhood: the wine had got into his head, the intoxication of rage and hatred blinded his saner judgment.

"Coward!" he shouted again and again.

His seconds tried to interpose, but he waved them feverishly aside. He would listen to no one. He saw no one save the man who had insulted Adèle, and who was heaping further insults upon her, by refusing this public acknowledgment of her virtues.

De Marny hated Déroulède at this moment with the most deadly hatred the heart of man can conceive. The older man's calm, his chivalry, his consideration only enhanced the boy's anger and shame.

The hubbub had become general. Everyone seemed carried away with this strange fever of enmity, which was seething in the Vicomte's veins. Most of the young men crowded round De Marny, doing their best to pacify him. The Marquis de Villefranche declared that the matter was getting quite outside the rules.

No one took much notice of Déroulède. In the remote corners of the saloon a few elderly dandies were laying bets as to the ultimate issue of the quarrel.

Déroulède, however, was beginning to lose his temper. He had no friends in that room, and therefore there was no sympathetic observer there, to note the gradual darkening of his eyes, like the gathering of a cloud heavy with the coming storm.

"I pray you, messieurs, let us cease the argument," he said at last, in a loud, impatient voice. "M. le Vicomte de Marny desires a further lesson, and, by God! he shall have it. En garde, M. le Vicomte!"

The crowd quickly drew back. The seconds once more assumed the bearing and imperturbable expression which their important function demanded. The hubbub ceased as the swords began to clash.

Everyone felt that farce was turning to tragedy.

And yet it was obvious from the first that Déroulède merely meant once more to disarm his antagonist, to give him one more lesson, a little more severe perhaps than the last. He was such a brilliant swordsman, and De Marny was so excited, that the advantage was with him from the very first.

How it all happened, nobody afterwards could say. There is no doubt that the little Vicomte's sword-play had become more and more wild: that he uncovered himself in the most reckless way, whilst lunging wildly at his opponent's breast, until at last, in one of these mad, unguarded moments, he seemed literally to throw himself upon Déroulède's weapon.

The latter tried with lightning-swift motion of the wrist to avoid the fatal issue, but it was too late, and without a sigh or groan, scarce a tremor, the Vicomte de Marny fell.

The sword dropped out of his hand, and it was Déroulède himself who caught the boy in his arms.

It had all occurred so quickly and suddenly that no one had realised it all, until it was over, and the lad was lying prone on the ground, his elegant blue satin coat stained with red, and his antagonist bending over him.

There was nothing more to be done. Etiquette demanded that Déroulède should withdraw. He was not allowed to do anything for the boy whom he had so unwillingly sent to his death.

As before, no one took much notice of him. Silence, the awesome silence caused by the presence of the great Master, fell upon all those around. Only in the far corner a shrill voice was heard to say:

"I hold you at five hundred louis, Marquis. The parvenu is a good swordsman."

The groups parted as Déroulède walked out of the room, followed by the Colonel and M. de Quettare, who stood by him to the last. Both were old and proved soldiers, both had chivalry and courage in them, with which to do tribute to the brave man whom they had seconded.

At the door of the establishment, they met the leech who had been summoned some little time ago to hold himself in readiness for any eventuality.

The great eventuality had occurred: it was beyond the leech's learning. In the brilliantly lighted saloon above, the only son of the Duc de Marny was breathing his last, whilst Déroulède, wrapping his mantle closely round him, strode out into the dark street, all alone.

II

The head of the house of Marny was at this time barely seventy years of age. But he had lived every hour, every minute of his life, from the day when the Grand Monarque gave him his first appointment as gentleman page in waiting when he was a mere lad, barely twelve years of age, to the moment—some ten years ago now—when Nature's relentless hand struck him down in the midst of his pleasures, withered him in a flash as she does a sturdy old oak, and nailed him— a cripple, almost a dotard—to the invalid chair which he would only quit for his last resting place.

Juliette was then a mere slip of a girl, an old man's child, the spoilt darling of his last happy years. She had retained some of the melancholy which had characterised her mother, the gentle lady who had endured so much so patiently, and who had bequeathed this final tender burden—her baby girl—to the brilliant, handsome husband whom she had so deeply loved, and so often forgiven.

When the Duc de Marny entered the final awesome stage of his gilded career, that deathlike life which he dragged on for ten years wearily to the grave, Juliette became his only joy, his one gleam of happiness in the midst of torturing memories.

In her deep, tender eyes he would see mirrored the present, the future for her, and would forget his past, with all its gaieties, its mad, merry years, that meant nothing now but bitter regrets, and endless rosary of the might-have-beens.

And then there was the boy. The little Vicomte, the future Duc de Marny, who would in his life and with his youth recreate the glory of the family, and make France once more ring with the echo of brave deeds and gallant adventures, which had made the name of Marny so glorious in camp and court.

The Vicomte was not his father's love, but he was his father's pride, and from the depths of his huge, cushioned arm-chair, the old man would listen with delight to stories from Versailles and Paris, the young Queen and the fascinating Lamballe, the latest play and the newest star in the theatrical firmament. His feeble, tottering mind would then take him back, along the paths of memory, to his own youth and his own triumphs, and in the joy and pride in his son, he would forget himself for the sake of the boy.

When they brought the Vicomte home that night, Juliette was the first to wake. She heard the noise outside the great gates, the coach slowly drawing up, the ring for the doorkeeper, and the sound of Matthieu's mutterings, who never liked to be called up in the middle of the night to let anyone through the gates.

Somehow a presentiment of evil at once struck the young girl: the footsteps sounded so heavy and muffled along the flagged courtyard, and up the great oak staircase. It seemed as if they were carrying something heavy, something inert or dead.

She jumped out of bed and hastily wrapped a cloak round her thin girlish shoulders, and slipped her feet into a pair of heelless shoes, then she opened her bedroom door and looked out upon the landing.

Two men, whom she did not know, were walking upstairs abreast, two more were carrying a heavy burden, and Matthieu was behind moaning and crying bitterly.

Juliette did not move. She stood in the doorway rigid as a statue. The little cortège went past her. No one saw her, for the landings in the Hotel de Marny are very wide, and Matthieu's lantern only threw a dim, flickering light upon the floor.

The men stopped outside the Vicomte's room. Matthieu opened it, and then the five men disappeared within, with their heavy burden.

A moment later old Pétronelle, who had been Juliette's nurse, and was now her devoted slave, came to her, all bathed in tears.

She had just heard the news, and she could scarcely speak, but she folded the young girl, her dear pet lamb, in her arms, and rocking herself to and fro she sobbed and eased her aching, motherly heart.

But Juliette did not cry. It was all so sudden, so awful. She, at fourteen years of age, had never dreamed of death; and now there was her brother, her Philippe, in whom she had so much joy, so much pride —he was dead—and her father must be told ...

The awfulness of this task seemed to Juliette like unto the last Judgment Day; a thing so terrible, so appalling, so impossible, that it would take a host of angels to proclaim its inevitableness.

The old cripple, with one foot in the grave, whose whole feeble mind, whose pride, whose final flicker of hope was concentrated in his boy, must be told that the lad had been brought home dead.

"Will you tell him, Pétronelle?" she asked repeatedly, during the brief intervals when the violence of the old nurse's grief subsided somewhat.

"No—no—darling, I cannot—I cannot—" moaned Pétronelle, amidst a renewed shower of sobs.

Juliette's entire soul—a child's soul it was—rose in revolt at thought of what was before her. She felt angered with God for having put such a thing upon her. What right had He to demand a girl of her years to endure so much mental agony?

To lose her brother, and to witness her father's grief! She couldn't! she couldn't! she couldn't! God was evil and unjust!

A distant tinkle of a bell made all her nerves suddenly quiver. Her father was awake then? He had heard the noise, and was ringing his bell to ask for an explanation of the disturbance.

With one quick movement Juliette jerked herself free from the nurse's arms, and before Pétronelle could prevent her, she had run out of the room, straight across the dark landing to a large panelled door opposite.

The old Duc de Marny was sitting on the edge of his bed, with his long, thin legs dangling helplessly to the ground.

Crippled as he was, he had struggled to this upright position, he was making frantic, miserable efforts to raise himself still further. He, too, had heard the dull thud of feet, the shuffling gait of men when carrying a heavy burden.

His mind flew back half-a-century, to the days when he had witnessed scenes wherein he was then merely a half-interested spectator. He knew the cortège composed of valets and friends, with the leech walking beside that precious burden, which anon would be deposited on the bed and left to the tender care of a mourning family.

Who knows what pictures were conjured up before that enfeebled vision? But he guessed. And when Juliette dashed into his room and stood before him, pale, trembling, a world of misery in her great eyes, she knew that he guessed and that she need not tell him. God had already done that for her.

Pierre, the old Duc's devoted valet, dressed him as quickly as he could. M. le Duc insisted on having his habit de cérémonie, the rich suit of black velvet with the priceless lace and diamond buttons, which he had worn when they laid le Roi Soleil to his eternal rest.

He put on his orders and buckled on his sword. The gorgeous clothes, which had suited him so well in the prime of his manhood, hung somewhat loosely on his attenuated frame, but he looked a grand and imposing figure, with his white hair tied behind with a great black bow, and the fine jabot of beautiful point d'Angleterre falling in a soft cascade below his chin.

Then holding himself as upright as he could, he sat in his invalid chair, and four flunkeys in full livery carried him to the deathbed of his son.

All the house was astir by now. Torches burned in great sockets in the vast hall and along the massive oak stairway, and hundreds of candles flickered ghostlike in the vast apartments of the princely mansion.

The numerous servants were arrayed on the landing, all dressed in the rich livery of the ducal house.

The death of an heir of the Marnys is an event that history makes a note of.

The old Duc's chair was placed close to the bed, where lay the dead body of the young Vicomte. He made no movement, nor did he utter a word or sigh. Some of those who were present at the time declared that his mind had completely given way, and that he neither felt nor understood the death of his son.

The Marquis de Villefranche, who had followed his friend to the last, took a final leave of the sorrowing house.

Juliette scarcely noticed him. Her eyes were fixed on her father. She would not look at her brother. A childlike fear had seized her, there, suddenly, between these two silent figures: the living and the dead.

But just as the Marquis was leaving the room, the old man spoke for the first time.

"Marquis," he said very quietly, "you forget—you have not yet told me who killed my son."

"It was in a fair fight, M. de Duc," replied the young Marquis, awed in spite of all his frivolity, his light-heartedness, by this strange, almost mysterious tragedy.

"Who killed my son, M. le Marquis?" repeated the old man mechanically. "I have the right to know," he added with sudden, weird energy.

"It was M. Paul Déroulède, M. le Duc," replied the Marquis. "I repeat, it was in fair fight."

The old Duc sighed as if in satisfaction. Then with a courteous gesture of farewell reminiscent of the grand siècle he added:

"All thanks from me and mine to you, Marquis, would seem but a mockery. Your devotion to my son is beyond human thanks. I'll not detain you now. Farewell."

Escorted by two lacqueys, the Marquis passed out of the room.

"Dismiss all the servants, Juliette; I have something to say," said the old Duc, and the young girl, silent, obedient, did as her father bade her.

Father and sister were alone with their dead. As soon as the last hushed footsteps of the retreating servants died away in the distance, the Duc de Marny seemed to throw away the lethargy which had enveloped him until now. With a quick, feverish gesture he seized his daughter's wrist, and murmured excitedly:

"His name. You heard his name, Juliette?"

"Yes, father," replied the child.

"Paul Déroulède! Paul Déroulède! You'll not forget it?"

"Never, father!"

"He killed your brother! You understand that? Killed my only son, the hope of my house, the last descendant of the most glorious race that has ever added lustre to the history of France."

"In fair fight, father!" protested the child.

"'Tis not fair for a man to kill a boy," retorted the old man, with furious energy.

"Déroulède is thirty: my boy was scarce out of his teens: may the vengeance of God fall upon the murderer!"

Juliette, awed, terrified, was gazing at her father with great, wondering eyes. He seemed unlike himself. His face wore a curious expression of ecstasy and of hatred, also of hope and exultation, whenever he looked steadily at her.

That the final glimmer of a tottering reason was fast leaving the poor, aching head she was too young to realise. Madness was a word that had only a vague meaning for her. Though she did not understand her father at the present moment, though she was half afraid of him, she would have rejected with scorn and horror any suggestion that he was mad.

Therefore when he took her hand and, drawing her nearer to the bed and to himself, placed it upon her dead brother's breast, she recoiled at the touch of the inanimate body, so unlike anything she had ever touched before, but she obeyed her father without any question, and listened to his words as to those of a sage.

"Juliette, you are now fourteen, and able to understand what I am going to ask of you. If I were not chained to this miserable chair, if I were not a hopeless, abject cripple, I would not depute anyone, not even you, my only child, to do that, which God demands that one of us should do."

He paused a moment, then continued earnestly:

"Remember, Juliette, that you are of the house of Marny, that you are a Catholic, and that God hears you now. For you shall swear an oath before Him and me, an oath from which only death can relieve you. Will you swear, my child?"

"If you wish it, father."

"You have been to confession lately, Juliette?"

"Yes, father; also to holy communion, yesterday," replied the child. "It was the Fête-Dieu, you know."

"Then you are in a state of grace, my child?"

"I was yesterday morning, father," replied the young girl naïvely, "but I have committed some little sins since then."

"Then make your confession to God in your heart now. You must be in a state of grace when you speak the oath."

The child closed her eyes, and as the old man watched her, he could see the lips framing the words of her spiritual confession.

Juliette made the sign of the cross, then opened her eyes and looked at her father.

"I am ready, father," she said; "I hope God has forgiven me the little sins of yesterday."

"Will you swear, my child?"

"What, father?"

"That you will avenge your brother's death on his murderer?"

"But, father ..."

"Swear it, my child!"

"How can I fulfil that oath, father?—I don't understand ..."

"God will guide you, my child. When you are older you will understand."

For a moment Juliette still hesitated. She was just on that borderland between childhood and womanhood when all the sensibilities, the nervous system, the emotions, are strung to their highest pitch.

Throughout her short life she had worshipped her father with a whole-hearted, passionate devotion, which had completely

xvi

blinded her to his weakening faculties and the feebleness of his mind.

She was also in that initial stage of enthusiastic piety which overwhelms every girl of temperament, if she be brought up in the Roman Catholic religion, when she is first initiated into the mysteries of the Sacraments.

Juliette had been to confession and communion. She had been confirmed by Monseigneur, the Archbishop. Her ardent nature had responded to the full to the sensuous and ecstatic expressions of the ancient faith.

And somehow her father's wish, her brother's death, all seemed mingled in her brain with that religion, for which in her juvenile enthusiasm she would willingly have laid down her life.

She thought of all the saints, whose lives she had been reading. Her young heart quivered at the thought of their sacrifices, their martyrdoms, their sense of duty.

An exaltation, morbid perhaps, superstitious and overwhelming, took possession of her mind; also, perhaps, far back in the innermost recesses of her heart, a pride in her own importance, her mission in life, her individuality: for she was a girl after all, a mere child, about to become a woman.

But the old Duc was waxing impatient.

"Surely you do not hesitate, Juliette, with your dead brother's body clamouring mutely for revenge? You, the only Marny left now!—for from this day I too shall be as dead."

"No, father," said the young girl in an awed whisper, "I do not hesitate. I will swear, just as you bid me."

"Repeat the words after me, my child."

"Yes, father."

"Before the face of Almighty God, who sees and hears me ..."

"Before the face of Almighty God, who sees and hears me," repeated Juliette firmly.

"I swear that I will seek out Paul Déroulède."

"I swear that I will seek out Paul Déroulède."

"And in any manner which God may dictate to me encompass his death, his ruin or dishonour, in revenge for my brother's death."

"And in any manner which God may dictate to me encompass his death, his ruin or dishonour, in revenge for my brother's death," said Juliette solemnly.

"May my brother's soul remain in torment until the final Judgment Day if I should break my oath, but may it rest in eternal peace the day on which his death is fitly avenged."

"May my brother's soul remain in torment until the final

Judgment Day if I should break my oath, but may it rest in eternal peace the day on which his death is fitly avenged."

The child fell upon her knees. The oath was spoken, the old man was satisfied.

He called for his valet, and allowed himself quietly to be put to bed.

One brief hour had transformed a child into a woman. A dangerous transformation when the brain is overburdened with emotions, when the nerves are overstrung and the heart full to breaking.

For the moment, however, the childlike nature reasserted itself for the last time, for Juliette, sobbing, had fled out of the room, to the privacy of her own apartment, and thrown herself passionately into the arms of kind old Pétronelle.

CHAPTER I

Paris: 1793

THE OUTRAGE

It would have been very difficult to say why Citizen Déroulède was quite so popular as he was. Still more difficult would it have been to state the reason why he remained immune from the prosecutions, which were being conducted at the rate of several scores a day, now against the moderate Gironde, anon against the fanatic Mountain, until the whole of France was transformed into one gigantic prison, that daily fed the guillotine.

But Déroulède remained unscathed. Even Merlin's law of the suspect had so far failed to touch him. And when, last July, the murder of Marat brought an entire holocaust of victims to the guillotine—from Adam Lux, who would have put up a statue in honour of Charlotte Corday, with the inscription: "Greater than Brutus", to Charlier, who would have had her publicly tortured and burned at the stake for her crime—Déroulède alone said nothing, and was allowed to remain silent.

The most seething time of that seething revolution. No one knew in the morning if his head would still be on his own shoulders in the evening, or if it would be held up by Citizen Samson the headsman, for the sansculottes of Paris to see.

Yet Déroulède was allowed to go his own way. Marat once said of him: "Il n'est pas dangereux." The phrase had been taken up. Within the precincts of the National Convention, Marat was still looked upon as the great protagonist of Liberty, a martyr to his own convictions carried to the extreme, to squalor and dirt, to the downward levelling of man to what is the lowest type in humanity. And his sayings were still treasured up: even the Girondins did not dare to attack his memory. Dead Marat was more powerful than his living presentment had been.

And he had said that Déroulède was not dangerous. Not dangerous to Republicanism, to liberty, to that downward, levelling process, the tearing down of old traditions, and the annihilation of past pretensions.

Déroulède had once been very rich. He had had sufficient prudence to give away in good time that which, undoubtedly, would have been taken away from him later on.

1

But when he gave willingly, at a time when France needed it most, and before she had learned how to help herself to what she wanted.

And somehow, in this instance, France had not forgotten: an invisible fortress seemed to surround Citizen Déroulède and keep his enemies at bay. They were few, but they existed. The National Convention trusted him. "He was not dangerous" to them. The people looked upon him as one of themselves, who gave whilst he had something to give. Who can gauge that most elusive of all things: Popularity?

He lived a quiet life, and had never yielded to the omni-prevalent temptation of writing pamphlets, but lived alone with his mother and Anne Mie, the little orphaned cousin whom old Madame Déroulède had taken care of, ever since the child could toddle.

Everyone knew his house in the Rue Ecole de Médecine, not far from the one wherein Marat lived and died, the only solid, stone house in the midst of a row of hovels, evil-smelling and squalid.

The street was narrow then, as it is now, and whilst Paris was cutting off the heads of her children for the sake of Liberty and Fraternity, she had no time to bother about cleanliness and sanitation.

Rue Ecole de Médecine did little credit to the school after which it was named, and it was a most unattractive crowd that usually thronged its uneven, muddy pavements.

A neat gown, a clean kerchief, were quite an unusual sight down this way, for Anne Mie seldom went out, and old Madame Déroulède hardly ever left her room. A good deal of brandy was being drunk at the two drinking bars, one at each end of the long, narrow street, and by five o'clock in the afternoon it was undoubtedly best for women to remain indoors.

The crowd of dishevelled elderly Amazons who stood gossiping at the street corner could hardly be called women now. A ragged petticoat, a greasy red kerchief round the head, a tattered, stained shift—to this pass of squalor and shame had Liberty brought the daughters of France.

And they jeered at any passer-by less filthy, less degraded than themselves.

"Ah! voyons l'aristo!" they shouted every time a man in decent clothes, a woman with tidy cap and apron, passed swiftly down the street.

And the afternoons were very lively. There was always plenty to see: first and foremost, the long procession of tumbrils, winding its way from the prisons to the Place de la Révolution. The forty-

2

four thousand sections of the Committee of Public Safety sent their quota, each in their turn, to the guillotine.

At one time these tumbrils contained royal ladies and gentlemen, ci-devant dukes and princesses, aristocrats from every county in France, but now this stock was becoming exhausted. The wretched Queen Marie Antoinette still lingered in the Temple with her son and daughter. Madame Elisabeth was still allowed to say her prayers in peace, but ci-devant dukes and counts were getting scarce: those who had not perished at the hand of Citizen Samson were plying some trade in Germany or England.

There were aristocratic joiners, innkeepers, and hairdressers. The proudest names in France were hidden beneath trade signs in London and Hamburg. A good number owed their lives to that mysterious Scarlet Pimpernel, that unknown Englishman who had snatched scores of victims from the clutches of Tinville the Prosecutor, and sent M. Chauvelin, baffled, back to France.

Aristocrats were getting scarce, so it was now the turn of deputies of the National Convention, of men of letters, men of science or of art, men who had sent others to the guillotine a twelvemonth ago, and men who had been loudest in defence of anarchy and its Reign of Terror.

They had revolutionised the Calendar: the Citizen-Deputies, and every good citizen of France, called this 19th day of August 1793 the 2nd Fructidor of the year I. of the New Era.

At six o'clock on that afternoon a young girl suddenly turned the angle of the Rue Ecole de Médecine, and after looking quickly to the right and left she began deliberately walking along the narrow street.

It was crowded just then. Groups of excited women stood jabbering before every doorway. It was the home-coming hour after the usual spectacle on the Place de la Révolution. The men had paused at the various drinking booths, crowding the women out. It would be the turn of these Amazons next, at the brandy bars; for the moment they were left to gossip, and to jeer at the passer-by.

At first the young girl did not seem to heed them. She walked quickly along, looking defiantly before her, carrying her head erect, and stepping carefully from cobblestone to cobblestone, avoiding the mud, which could have dirtied her dainty shoes.

The harridans passed the time of day to her, and the time of day meant some obscene remark unfit for women's ears. The young girl wore a simple grey dress, with fine lawn kerchief neatly folded across her bosom, a large hat with flowing ribbons sat above the fairest face that ever gladdened men's eyes to see.

3

Fairer still it would have been, but for the look of determination which made it seem hard and old for the girl's years.

She wore the tricolour scarf round her waist, else she had been more seriously molested ere now. But the Republican colours were her safeguard: whilst she walked quietly along, no one could harm her.

Then suddenly a curious impulse seemed to seize her. It was just outside the large stone house belonging to Citizen-Deputy Déroulède. She had so far taken no notice of the groups of women which she had come across. When they obstructed the footway, she had calmly stepped out into the middle of the road.

It was wise and prudent, for she could close her ears to obscene language and need pay no heed to insult.

Suddenly she threw up her head defiantly.

"Will you please let me pass?" she said loudly, as a dishevelled Amazon stood before her with arms akimbo, glancing sarcastically at the lace petticoat, which just peeped beneath the young girl's simple grey frock.

"Let her pass? Let her pass? Ho! ho! ho!" laughed the old woman, turning to the nearest group of idlers, and apostrophising them with a loud oath. "Did you know, citizeness, that this street had been specially made for aristos to pass along?"

"I am in a hurry, will you let me pass at once?" commanded the young girl, tapping her foot impatiently on the ground.

There was the whole width of the street on her right, plenty of room for her to walk along. It seemed positive madness to provoke a quarrel singlehanded against this noisy group of excited females, just home from the ghastly spectacle around the guillotine.

And yet she seemed to do it wilfully, as if coming to the end of her patience, all her proud, aristocratic blood in revolt against this evil-smelling crowd which surrounded her.

Half-tipsy men and noisome, naked urchins seemed to have sprung from everywhere.

"Oho, quelle aristo!" they shouted with ironical astonishment, gazing at the young girl's face, fingering her gown, thrusting begrimed, hate-distorted faces close to her own.

Instinctively she recoiled and backed towards the house immediately on her left. It was adorned with a porch made of stout oak beams, with a tiled roof; an iron lantern descended from this, and there was a stone parapet below, and a few steps, at right angles from the pavement, led up to the massive door.

On these steps the young girl had taken refuge. Proud, defiant, she confronted the howling mob, which she had so wilfully provoked.

4

"Of a truth, Citizeness Margot, that grey dress would become you well!" suggested a young man, whose red cap hung in tatters over an evil and dissolute-looking face.

"And all that fine lace would make a splendid jabot round the aristo's neck when Citizen Samson holds up her head for us to see," added another, as with mock elegance he stooped and with two very grimy fingers slightly raised the young girl's grey frock, displaying the lace-edged petticoat beneath.

A volley of oaths and loud, ironical laughter greeted this sally.

"'Tis mighty fine lace to be thus hidden away," commented an elderly harridan. "Now, would you believe it, my fine madam, but my legs are bare underneath my kirtle?"

"And dirty, too, I'll lay a wager," laughed another. "Soap is dear in Paris just now."

"The lace on the aristo's kerchief would pay the baker's bill of a whole family for a month!" shouted an excited voice.

Heat and brandy further addled the brains of this group of French citizens; hatred gleamed out of every eye. Outrage was imminent. The young girl seemed to know it, but she remained defiant and self-possessed, gradually stepping back and back up the steps, closely followed by her assailants.

"To the Jew with the gewgaw, then!" shouted a thin, haggard female viciously, as she suddenly clutched at the young girl's kerchief, and with a mocking, triumphant laugh tore it from her bosom.

This outrage seemed to be the signal for the breaking down of the final barriers which ordinary decency should have raised. The language and vituperation became such as no chronicler could record.

The girl's dainty white neck, her clear skin, the refined contour of shoulders and bust, seemed to have aroused the deadliest lust of hate in these wretched creatures, rendered bestial by famine and squalor.

It seemed almost as if one would vie with the other in seeking for words which would most offend these small aristocratic ears.

The young girl was now crouching against the doorway, her hands held up to her ears to shut out the awful sounds. She did not seem frightened, only appalled at the terrible volcano which she had provoked.

Suddenly a miserable harridan struck her straight in the face, with hard, grimy fist, and a long shout of exultation greeted this monstrous deed.

Then only did the girl seem to lose her self-control.

"A moi," she shouted loudly, whilst hammering with both

hands against the massive doorway. "A moi! Murder! Murder! Citoyen Déroulède, à moi!"

But her terror was greeted with renewed glee by her assailants. They were now roused to the highest point of frenzy: the crowd of brutes would in the next moment have torn the helpless girl from her place of refuge and dragged her into the mire, an outraged prey, for the satisfaction of an ungovernable hate.

But just as half-a-dozen pairs of talon-like hands clutched frantically at her skirts, the door behind her was quickly opened. She felt her arm seized firmly, and herself dragged swiftly within the shelter of the threshold.

Her senses, overwrought by the terrible adventure which she had just gone through, were threatening to reel; she heard the massive door close, shutting out the yells of baffled rage, the ironical laughter, the obscene words, which sounded in her ears like the shrieks of Dante's damned.

She could not see her rescuer, for the hall into which he had hastily dragged her was only dimly lighted. But a peremptory voice said quickly:

"Up the stairs, the room straight in front of you, my mother is there. Go quickly."

She had fallen on her knees, cowering against the heavy oak beam which supported the ceiling, and was straining her eyes to catch sight of the man, to whom at this moment she perhaps owed more than her life: but he was standing against the doorway, with his hand on the latch.

"What are you going to do?" she murmured.

"Prevent their breaking into my house in order to drag you out of it," he replied quietly; "so, I pray you, do as I bid you."

Mechanically she obeyed him, drew herself to her feet, and, turning towards the stairs, began slowly to mount the shallow steps. Her knees were shaking under her, her whole body was trembling with horror at the awesome crisis she had just traversed.

She dared not look back at her rescuer. Her head was bent, and her lips were murmuring half-audible words as she went.

Outside the hooting and yelling was becoming louder and louder. Enraged fists were hammering violently against the stout oak door.

At the top of the stairs, moved by an irresistible impulse, she turned and looked into the hall.

She saw his figure dimly outlined in the gloom, one hand on the latch, his head thrown back to watch her movements.

A door stood ajar immediately in front of her. She pushed it open and went within.

6

At that moment he too opened the door below. The shrieks of the howling mob once more resounded close to her ears. It seemed as if they had surrounded him. She wondered what was happening, and marvelled how he dared to face that awful crowd alone.

The room into which she had entered was gay and cheerful-looking with its dainty chintz hangings and graceful, elegant pieces of furniture. The young girl looked up, as a kindly voice said to her, from out the depths of a capacious armchair:

"Come in, come in, my dear, and close the door behind you! Did those wretches attack you? Never mind. Paul will speak to them. Come here, my dear, and sit down; there's no cause now for fear."

Without a word the young girl came forward. She seemed now to be walking in a dream, the chintz hangings to be swaying ghostlike around her, the yells and shrieks below to come from the very bowels of the earth.

The old lady continued to prattle on. She had taken the girl's hand in hers, and was gently forcing her down on to a low stool beside her armchair. She was talking about Paul, and said something about Anne Mie, and then about the National Convention, and those beasts and savages, but mostly about Paul.

The noise outside had subsided. The girl felt strangely sick and tired. Her head seemed to be whirling round, the furniture to be dancing round her; the old lady's face looked at her through a swaying veil, and then—and then ...

Tired Nature was having her way at last; she folded the quivering young body in her motherly arms, and wrapped the aching senses beneath her merciful mantle of unconsciousness.

CHAPTER II

CITIZEN-DEPUTY

When, presently, the young girl awoke, with a delicious feeling of rest and well-being, she had plenty of leisure to think.

So, then, this was his house! She was actually a guest, a rescued protégé, beneath the roof of Citoyen Déroulède.

He had dragged her from the clutches of the howling mob which she had provoked; his mother had made her welcome, a sweet-faced, young girl scarce out of her teens, sad-eyed and slightly deformed, had waited upon her and made her happy and comfortable.

Juliette de Marny was in the house of the man, whom she had sworn before her God and before her father to pursue with hatred and revenge.

Ten years had gone by since then.

Lying upon the sweet-scented bed which the hospitality of the Déroulèdes had provided for her, she seemed to see passing before her the spectres of these past ten years—the first four, after her brother's death, until the old Duc de Marny's body slowly followed his soul to its grave.

After that last glimmer of life beside the deathbed of his son, the old Duc had practically ceased to be. A mute, shrunken figure, he merely existed; his mind vanished, his memory gone, a wreck whom Nature fortunately remembered at last, and finally took away from the invalid chair which had been his world.

Then came those few years at the Convent of the Ursulines. Juliette had hoped that she had a vocation; her whole soul yearned for a secluded, a religious, life, for great barriers of solemn vows and days spent in prayer and contemplation, to interpose between herself and the memory of that awful night when, obedient to her father's will, she had made the solemn oath to avenge her brother's death.

She was only eighteen when she first entered the convent, directly after her father's death, when she felt very lonely—both morally and mentally lonely—and followed by the obsession of that oath.

She never spoke of it to anyone except to her confessor, and he, a simple-minded man of great learning and a total lack of knowledge of the world, was completely at a loss how to advise.

8

The Archbishop was consulted. He could grant a dispensation, and release her of that most solemn vow.

When first this idea was suggested to her, Juliette was exultant. Her entire nature, which in itself was wholesome, light-hearted, the very reverse of morbid, rebelled against this unnatural task placed upon her young shoulders. It was only religion—the strange, warped religion of that extraordinary age—which kept her to it, which forbade her breaking lightly that most unnatural oath.

The Archbishop was a man of many duties, many engagements. He agreed to give this strange "cas de conscience" his most earnest attention. He would make no promises. But Mademoiselle de Marny was rich: a munificent donation to the poor of Paris, or to some cause dear to the Holy Father himself, might perhaps be more acceptable to God than the fulfilment of a compulsory vow.

Juliette, within the convent walls, was waiting patiently for the Archbishop's decision at the very moment, when the greatest upheaval the world has ever known was beginning to shake the very foundations of France.

The Archbishop had other things now to think about than isolated cases of conscience. He forgot all about Juliette, probably. He was busy consoling a monarch for the loss of his throne, and preparing himself and his royal patron for the scaffold.

The Convent of the Ursulines was scattered during the Terror. Everyone remembers the Thermidor massacres, and the thirty-four nuns, all daughters of ancient families of France, who went so cheerfully to the scaffold.

Juliette was one of those who escaped condemnation. How or why, she herself could not have told. She was very young, and still a postulant; she was allowed to live in retirement with Pétronelle, her old nurse, who had remained faithful through all these years.

Then the Archbishop was prosecuted and imprisoned. Juliette made frantic efforts to see him, but all in vain. When he died, she looked upon her spiritual guide's death as a direct warning from God, that nothing could relieve her of her oath.

She had watched the turmoils of the Revolution through the attic window of her tiny apartment in Paris. Waited upon by faithful Pétronelle, she had been forced to live on the savings of that worthy old soul, as all her property, all the Marny estates, the dot she took with her to the convent—everything, in fact—had been seized by the Revolutionary Government, self appointed to level fortunes, as well as individuals.

From that attic window she had seen beautiful Paris writhing under the pitiless lash of the demon of terror which it had provoked;

9

she had heard the rumble of the tumbrils, dragging day after day their load of victims to the insatiable maker of this Revolution of Fraternity—the Guillotine.

She had seen the gay, light-hearted people of this Star-City turned to howling beasts of prey, its women changed to sexless vultures, with murderous talons implanted in everything that is noble, high or beautiful.

She was not twenty when the feeble, vacillating monarch and his imperious consort were dragged back—a pair of humiliated prisoners— to the capital from which they had tried to flee.

Two years later, she had heard the cries of an entire people exulting over a regicide. Then the murder of Marat, by a young girl like herself, the pale-faced, large-eyed Charlotte, who had committed a crime for the sake of a conviction. "Greater than Brutus!" some had called her. Greater than Joan of Arc, for it was to a mission of evil and of sin that she was called from the depths of her Breton village, and not to one of glory and triumph.

"Greater than Brutus!"

Juliette followed the trial of Charlotte Corday with all the passionate ardour of her exalted temperament.

Just think what an effect it must have had upon the mind of this young girl, who for nine years—the best of her life—had also lived with the idea of a sublime mission pervading her very soul.

She watched Charlotte Corday at her trial. Conquering her natural repulsion for such scenes, and the crowds which usually watched them, she had forced her way into the foremost rank of the narrow gallery which overlooked the Hall of the Revolutionary Tribunal.

She heard the indictment, heard Tinville's speech and the calling of the witnesses.

"All this is unnecessary. I killed Marat!"

Juliette heard the fresh young voice ringing out clearly above the murmur of voices, the howls of execration; she saw the beautiful young face, clear, calm, impassive.

"I killed Marat!"

And there in the special space allotted to the Citizen-Deputies, sitting among those who represented the party of the Moderate Gironde, was Paul Déroulède, the man whom she had sworn to pursue with a vengeance as great, as complete, as that which guided Charlotte Corday's hand.

She watched him during the trial, and wondered if he had any presentiment of the hatred which dogged him, like unto the one which had dogged Marat.

He was very dark, almost swarthy a son of the South, with

10

brown hair, free from powder, thrown back and revealing the brow of a student rather than that of a legislator. He watched Charlotte Corday earnestly, and Juliette who watched him saw the look of measureless pity, which softened the otherwise hard look of his close-set eyes.

He made an impassioned speech for the defence: a speech which has become historic. It would have cost any other man his head.

Juliette marvelled at his courage; to defend Charlotte Corday was equivalent to acquiescing in the death of Marat: Marat, the friend of the people; Marat, whom his funeral orators had compared to the Great, the Sacred Leveller of Mankind!

But Déroulède's speech was not a defence, it was an appeal. The most eloquent man of that eloquent age, his words seemed to find that hidden bit of sentiment which still lurked in the hearts of these strange protagonists of Hate.

Everyone round Juliette listened as he spoke: "It is Citoyen Déroulède!" whispered the bloodthirsty Amazons, who sat knitting in the gallery.

But there was no further comment. A huge, magnificently-equipped hospital for sick children had been thrown open in Paris that very morning, a gift to the nation from Citoyen Déroulède. Surely he was privileged to talk a little, if it pleased him. His hospital would cover quite a good many defalcations.

Even the rabid Mountain, Danton, Merlin, Santerre, shrugged their shoulders. "It is Déroulède, let him talk an he list. Murdered Marat said of him that he was not dangerous."

Juliette heard it all. The knitters round her were talking loudly. Even Charlotte was almost forgotten whilst Déroulède talked. He had a fine voice, of strong calibre, which echoed powerfully through the hall.

He was rather short, but broad-shouldered and well knit, with an expressive hand, which looked slender and delicate below the fine lace ruffle.

Charlotte Corday was condemned. All Déroulède's eloquence could not save her.

Juliette left the court in a state of mad exultation. She was very young: the scenes she had witnessed in the past two years could not help but excite the imagination of a young girl, left entirely to her own intellectual and moral resources.

What scenes! Great God!

And now to wait for an opportunity! Charlotte Corday, the half-educated little provincial should not put to shame

11

Mademoiselle de Marny, the daughter of a hundred dukes, of those who had made France before she took to unmaking herself.

But she could not formulate any definite plans. Pétronelle, poor old soul, her only confidante, was not of the stuff that heroines are made of. Juliette felt impelled by duty, and duty at best is not so prompt a counsellor as love or hate.

Her adventure outside Déroulède's house had not been premeditated. Impulse and coincidence had worked their will with her.

She had been in the habit, daily, for the past month, of wandering down the Rue Ecole de Médecine, ostensibly to gaze at Marat's dwelling, as crowds of idlers were wont to do, but really in order to look at Déroulède's house. Once or twice she saw him coming or going from home. Once she caught sight of the inner hall, and of a young girl in a dark kirtle and snow-white kerchief bidding him good-bye at his door. Another time she caught sight of him at the corner of the street, helping that same young girl over the muddy pavement. He had just met her, and she was carrying a basket of provisions: he took it from her and carried it to the house.

Chivalrous—eh?—and innately so, evidently, for the girl was slightly deformed: hardly a hunchback, but weak and unattractive-looking, with melancholy eyes, and a pale, pinched face.

It was the thought of that little act of simple chivalry, witnessed the day before, which caused Juliette to provoke the scene which, but for Déroulède's timely interference, might have ended so fatally. But she reckoned on that interference: the whole thing had occurred to her suddenly, and she had carried it through.

Had not her father said to her that when the time came, God would show her a means to the end?

And now she was inside the house of the man who had murdered her brother and sent her sorrowing father, a poor, senseless maniac, tottering to the grave.

Would God's finger point again, and show her what to do next, how best to accomplish what she had sworn to do?

CHAPTER III

HOSPITALITY

"Is there anything more I can do for you now, mademoiselle?"

The gentle, timid voice roused Juliette from the contemplation of the past.

She smiled at Anne Mie, and held her hand out towards her.

"You have all been so kind," she said, "I want to get up now and thank you all."

"Don't move unless you feel quite well."

"I am quite well now. Those horrid people frightened me so, that is why I fainted."

"They would have half-killed you, if ..."

"Will you tell me where I am?" asked Juliette.

"In the house of M. Paul Déroulède—I should have said of Citizen-Deputy Déroulède. He rescued you from the mob, and pacified them. He has such a beautiful voice that he can make anyone listen to him, and ..."

"And you are fond of him, mademoiselle?" added Juliette, suddenly feeling a mist of tears rising to her eyes.

"Of course I am fond of him," rejoined the other girl simply, whilst a look of the most tender-hearted devotion seemed to beautify her pale face. "He and Madame Déroulède have brought me up; I never knew my parents. They have cared for me, and he has taught me all I know."

"What do they call you, mademoiselle?"

"My name is Anne Mie."

"And mine, Juliette—Juliette Marny," she added after a slight hesitation. "I have no parents either. My old nurse, Pétronelle, has brought me up, and—But tell me more about M. Déroulède—I owe him so much, I'd like to know him better."

"Will you not let me arrange your hair?" said Anne Mie as if purposely evading a direct reply. "M. Déroulède is in the salon with madame. You can see him then."

Juliette asked no more questions, but allowed Anne Mie to tidy her hair for her, to lend her a fresh kerchief and generally to efface all traces of her terrible adventure. She felt puzzled and tearful. Anne Mie's gentleness seemed somehow to jar on her spirits. She could not understand the girl's position in the Déroulède

13

household. Was she a relative, or a superior servant? In these troublous times she might easily have been both.

In any case she was a childhood's companion of the Citizen-Deputy— whether on an equal or a humbler footing, Juliette would have given much to ascertain.

With the marvellous instinct peculiar to women of temperament, she had already divined Anne Mie's love for Déroulède. The poor young cripple's very soul seemed to quiver magnetically at the bare mention of his name, her whole face became transfigured: Juliette even thought her beautiful then.

She looked at herself critically in the glass, and adjusted a curl, which looked its best when it was rebellious. She scrutinised her own face carefully; why? she could not tell: another of those subtle feminine instincts perhaps.

The becoming simplicity of the prevailing mode suited her to perfection. The waist line, rather high but clearly defined—a precursor of the later more accentuated fashion—gave grace to her long slender limbs, and emphasised the lissomeness of her figure. The kerchief, edged with fine lace, and neatly folded across her bosom, softened the contour of her girlish bust and shoulders.

And her hair was a veritable glory round her dainty, piquant face. Soft, fair, and curly, it emerged in a golden halo from beneath the prettiest little lace cap imaginable.

She turned and faced Anne Mie, ready to follow her out of the room, and the young crippled girl sighed as she smoothed down the folds of her own apron, and gave a final touch to the completion of Juliette's attire.

The time before the evening meal slipped by like a dream-hour for Juliette.

She had lived so much alone, had led such an introspective life, that she had hardly realised and understood all that was going on around her. At the time when the inner vitality of France first asserted itself and then swept away all that hindered its mad progress, she was tied to the invalid chair of her half-demented father; then, after that, the sheltering walls of the Ursuline Convent had hidden from her mental vision the true meaning of the great conflict, between the Old Era and the New.

Déroulède was neither a pedant nor yet a revolutionary: his theories were Utopian and he had an extraordinary overpowering sympathy for his fellow-men.

After the first casual greetings with Juliette, he had continued a discussion with his mother, which the young girl's entrance had interrupted.

14

He seemed to take but little notice of her, although at times his dark, keen eyes would seek hers, as if challenging her for a reply.

He was talking of the mob of Paris, whom he evidently understood so well. Incidents such as the one which Juliette had provoked, had led to rape and theft, often to murder, before now: but outside Citizen-Deputy Déroulède's house everything was quiet, half-an-hour after Juliette's escape from that howling, brutish crowd.

He had merely spoken to them, for about twenty minutes, and they had gone away quite quietly, without even touching one hair of his head. He seemed to love them: to know how to separate the little good that was in them, from that hard crust of evil, which misery had put around their hearts.

Once he addressed Juliette somewhat abruptly: "Pardon me, mademoiselle, but for your own sake we must guard you a prisoner here awhile. No one would harm you under this roof, but it would not be safe for you to cross the neighbouring streets to-night."

"But I must go, monsieur. Indeed, indeed I must!" she said earnestly. "I am deeply grateful to you, but I could not leave Pétronelle."

"Who is Pétronelle?"

"My dear old nurse, monsieur. She has never left me. Think how anxious and miserable she must be, at my prolonged absence."

"Where does she live?"

"At No. 15 Rue Taitbout, but ..."

"Will you allow me to take her a message?—telling her that you are safe and under my roof, where it is obviously more prudent that you should remain at present."

"If you think it best, monsieur," she replied.

Inwardly she was trembling with excitement. God had not only brought her to this house, but willed that she should stay in it.

"In whose name shall I take the message, mademoiselle?" he asked.

"My name is Juliette Marny."

She watched him keenly as she said it, but there was not the slightest sign in his expressive face, to show that he had recognised the name.

Ten years is a long time, and every one had lived through so much during those years! A wave of intense wrath swept through Juliette's soul, as she realised that he had forgotten. The name meant nothing to him! It did not recall to him the fact that his hand was stained with blood. During ten years she had suffered, she had fought with herself, fought for him as it were, against the Fate which

15

she was destined to mete out to him, whilst he had forgotten, or at least had ceased to think.

He bowed to her and went out of the room.

The wave of wrath subsided, and she was left alone with Madame Déroulède: presently Anne Mie came in.

The three women chatted together, waiting for the return of the master of the house. Juliette felt well and, in spite of herself, almost happy. She had lived so long in the miserable, little attic alone with Pétronelle that she enjoyed the well-being of this refined home. It was not so grand or gorgeous of course as her father's princely palace opposite the Louvre, a wreck now, since it was annexed by the Committee of National Defence, for the housing of soldiery. But the Déroulèdes' home was essentially a refined one. The delicate china on the tall chimney-piece, the few bits of Buhl and Vernis Martin about the room, the vision through the open doorway of the supper-table spread with a fine white cloth, and sparkling with silver, all spoke of fastidious tastes, of habits of luxury and elegance, which the spirit of Equality and Anarchy had not succeeded in eradicating.

When Déroulède came back, he brought an atmosphere of breezy cheerfulness with him.

The street was quiet now, and when walking past the hospital—his own gift to the Nation—he had been loudly cheered. One or two ironical voices had asked him what he had done with the aristo and her lace furbelows, but it remained at that and Mademoiselle Marny need have no fear.

He had brought Pétronelle along with him: his careless, lavish hospitality would have suggested the housing of Juliette's entire domestic establishment, had she possessed one.

As it was, the worthy old soul's deluge of happy tears had melted his kindly heart. He offered her and her young mistress shelter, until the small cloud should have rolled by.

After that he suggested a journey to England. Emigration now was the only real safety, and Mademoiselle Marny had unpleasantly drawn on herself the attention of the Paris rabble. No doubt, within the next few days her name would figure among the "suspect." She would be safest out of the country, and could not do better than place herself under the guidance of that English enthusiast, who had helped so many persecuted Frenchmen to escape from the terrors of the Revolution: the man who was such a thorn in the flesh of the Committee of Public Safety, and who went by the nickname of The Scarlet Pimpernel.

CHAPTER IV

THE FAITHFUL HOUSE-DOG

After supper they talked of Charlotte Corday.

Juliette clung to the vision of that heroine, and liked to talk of her. She appeared as a justification of her own actions, which somehow seemed to require justification.

She loved to hear Paul Déroulède talk; liked to provoke his enthusiasm and to see his stern, dark face light up with the inward fire of the enthusiast.

She had openly avowed herself as the daughter of the Duc de Marny. When she actually named her father, and her brother killed in duel, she saw Déroulède looking long and searchingly at her. Evidently he wondered if she knew everything: but she returned his gaze fearlessly and frankly, and he apparently was satisfied.

Madame Déroulède seemed to know nothing of the circumstances of that duel. Déroulède tried to draw Juliette out, to make her speak of her brother. She replied to his questions quite openly, but there was nothing in what she said, suggestive of the fact that she knew who killed her brother.

She wanted him to know who she was. If he feared an enemy in her, there was yet time enough for him to close his doors against her.

But less than a minute later, he had renewed his warmest offers of hospitality.

"Until we can arrange for your journey to England," he added with a short sigh, as if reluctant to part from her.

To Juliette his attitude seemed one of complete indifference for the wrong he had done to her and to her father: feeling that she was an avenging spirit, with flaming sword in hand, pursuing her brother's murderer like a relentless Nemesis, she would have preferred to see him cowed before her, even afraid of her, though she was only a young and delicate girl.

She did not understand that in the simplicity of his heart, he only wished to make amends. The quarrel with the young Vicomte de Marny had been forced upon him, the fight had been honourable and fair, and on his side fought with every desire to spare the young man. He had merely been the instrument of Fate, but he felt happy that Fate once more used him as her tool, this time to save the sister.

Whilst Déroulède and Juliette talked together Anne Mie cleared the supper-table, then came and sat on a low stool at madame's feet. She took no part in the conversation, but every now and then Juliette felt the girl's melancholy eyes fixed almost reproachfully upon her.

When Juliette had retired with Pétronelle, Déroulède took Anne Mie's hand in his.

"You will be kind to my guest, Anne Mie, won't you? She seems very lonely, and has gone through a great deal."

"Not more than I have," murmured the young girl involuntarily.

"You are not happy, Anne Mie? I thought ..."

"Is a wretched, deformed creature ever happy?" she said with sudden vehemence, as tears of mortification rushed to her eyes, in spite of herself.

"I did not think that you were wretched," he replied with some sadness, "and neither in my eyes, nor in my mother's, are you in any way deformed."

Her mood changed at once. She clung to him, pressing his hand between her own.

"Forgive me! I—I don't know what's the matter with me to-night," she said with a nervous little laugh. "Let me see, you asked me to be kind to Mademoiselle Marny, did you not?"

He nodded with a smile.

"Of course I'll be kind to her. Isn't every one kind to one who is young and beautiful, and has great, appealing eyes, and soft, curly hair? Ah me! how easy is the path in life for some people! What do you want me to do, Paul? Wait on her? Be her little maid? Soothe her nerves or what? I'll do it all, though in her eyes I shall remain both wretched and deformed, a creature to pity, the harmless, necessary house-dog ..."

She paused a moment: said "Good-night" to him, and turned to go, candle in hand, looking pathetic and fragile, with that ugly contour of shoulder, which Déroulède assured her he could not see.

The candle flickered in the draught, illumining the thin, pinched face, the large melancholy eyes of the faithful house-dog.

"Who can watch and bite!" she said half-audibly as she slipped out of the room. "For I do not trust you, my fine madam, and there was something about that comedy this afternoon, which somehow, I don't quite understand."

CHAPTER V

A DAY IN THE WOODS

But whilst men and women set to work to make the towns of France hideous with their shrieks and their hootings, their mock-trials and bloody guillotines, they could not quite prevent Nature from working her sweet will with the country.

June, July, and August had received new names—they were now called Messidor, Thermidor, and Fructidor, but under these new names they continued to pour forth upon the earth the same old fruits, the same flowers, the same grass in the meadows and leaves upon the trees.

Messidor brought its quota of wild roses in the hedgerows, just as archaic June had done. Thermidor covered the barren cornfields with its flaming mantle of scarlet poppies, and Fructidor, though now called August, still tipped the wild sorrel with dots of crimson, and laid the first wash of tender colour on the pale cheeks of the ripening peaches.

And Juliette—young, girlish, feminine and inconsequent—had sighed for country and sunshine, had longed for a ramble in the woods, the music of the birds, the sight of the meadows sugared with marguerites.

She had left the house early: accompanied by Pétronelle, she had been rowed along the river as far as Suresnes. They had brought some bread and fresh butter, a little wine and fruit in a basket, and from here she meant to wander homewards through the woods.

It was all so peaceful, so remote: even the noise of shrieking, howling Paris did not reach the leafy thickets of Suresnes.

It almost seemed as if this little old-world village had been forgotten by the destroyers of France. It had never been a royal residence, the woods had never been preserved for royal sport: there was no vengeance to be wreaked upon its peaceful glades and sleepy, fragrant meadows.

Juliette spent a happy day; she loved the flowers, the trees, the birds, and Pétronelle was silent and sympathetic. As the afternoon wore on, and it was time to go home, Juliette turned townwards with a sigh.

You all know that road through the woods, which lies to the north-west of Paris: so leafy, so secluded. No large, hundred-year-old trees, no fine oaks or antique elms, but numberless delicate

19

stems of hazel-nut and young ash, covered with honeysuckle at this time of year, sweet-smelling and so peaceful after that awful turmoil of the town.

Obedient to Madame Déroulède's suggestion, Juliette had tied a tricolour scarf round her waist, and a Phrygian cap of crimson cloth, with the inevitable rosette on one side, adorned her curly head.

She had gathered a huge bouquet of poppies, marguerites and blue lupin —Nature's tribute to the national colours—and as she wandered through the sylvan glades she looked like some quaint dweller of the woods—a sprite, mayhap—with old mother Pétronelle trotting behind her, like an attendant witch.

Suddenly she paused, for in the near distance she had perceived the sound of footsteps upon the leafy turf, and the next moment Paul Déroulède emerged from out the thicket and came rapidly towards her.

"We were so anxious about you at home!" he said, almost by way of an apology. "My mother became so restless ..."

"That to quiet her fears you came in search of me!" she retorted with a gay little laugh, the laugh of a young girl, scarce a woman as yet, who feels that she is good to look at, good to talk to, who feels her wings for the first time, the wings with which to soar into that mad, merry, elusive land called Romance. Ay, her wings! but her power also! that sweet, subtle power of the woman: the yoke which men love, rail at, and love again, the yoke that enslaves them and gives them the joy of kings.

How happy the day had been! Yet it had been incomplete!

Pétronelle was somewhat dull, and Juliette was too young to enjoy long companionship with her own thoughts. Now suddenly the day seemed to have become perfect. There was someone there to appreciate the charm of the woods, the beauty of that blue sky peeping though the tangled foliage of the honeysuckle-covered trees. There was some one to talk to, someone to admire the fresh white frock Juliette had put on that morning.

"But how did you know where to find me?" she asked with a quaint touch of immature coquetry.

"I didn't know," he replied quietly. "They told me you had gone to Suresness, and meant to wander homewards through the woods. It frightened me, for you will have to go through the north-west barrier, and ..."

"Well?"

He smiled, and looked earnestly for a moment at the dainty apparition before him.

"Well, you know!" he said gaily, "that tricolour scarf and the

20

red cap are not quite sufficient as a disguise: you look anything but a staunch friend of the people. I guessed that your muslin frock would be clean, and that there would still be some tell-tale lace upon it."

She laughed again, and with delicate fingers lifted her pretty muslin frock, displaying a white frou-frou of flounces beneath the hem.

"How careless and childish!" he said, almost roughly.

"Would you have me coarse and grimy to be a fitting match for your partisans?" she retorted.

His tone of mentor nettled her, his attitude seemed to her priggish and dictatorial, and as the sun disappearing behind a sudden cloud, so her childish merriment quickly gave place to a feeling of unexplainable disappointment.

"I humbly beg your pardon," he said quietly, "And must crave your kind indulgence for my mood: but I have been so anxious ..."

"Why should you be anxious about me?"

She had meant to say this indifferently, as if caring little what the reply might be: but in her effort to seem indifferent her voice became haughty, a reminiscence of the days when she still was the daughter of the Duc de Marny, the richest and most high-born heiress in France.

"Was that presumptuous?" he asked, with a slight touch of irony, in response to her own hauteur.

"It was merely unnecessary," she replied. "I have already laid too many burdens on your shoulders, without wishing to add that of anxiety."

"You have laid no burden on me," he said quietly, "save one of gratitude."

"Gratitude? What have I done?"

"You committed a foolish, thoughtless act outside my door, and gave me the chance of easing my conscience of a heavy load."

"In what way?"

"I had never hoped that the Fates would be so kind as to allow me to render a member of your family a slight service."

"I understand that you saved my life the other day, Monsieur Déroulède. I know that I am still in peril and that I owe my safety to you ..."

"Do you also know that your brother owed his death to me?"

She closed her lips firmly, unable to reply, wrathful with him, for having suddenly and without any warning, placed a clumsy hand upon that hidden sore.

"I always meant to tell you," he continued somewhat hurriedly; "for it almost seemed to me that I have been cheating

21

you, these last few days. I don't suppose that you can quite realise what it means to me to tell you this just now; but I owe it to you, I think. In later years you might find out, and then regret the days you spent under my roof. I called you childish a moment ago, you must forgive me; I know that you are a woman, and hope therefore that you will understand me. I killed your brother in fair fight. He provoked me as no man was ever provoked before ..."

"Is it necessary, M. Déroulède, that you should tell me all this?" she interrupted him with some impatience.

"I thought you ought to know."

"You must know, on the other hand, that I have no means of hearing the history of the quarrel from my brother's point of view now."

The moment the words were out of her lips she had realised how cruelly she had spoken. He did not reply; he was too chivalrous, too gentle, to reproach her. Perhaps he understood for the first time how bitterly she had felt her brother's death, and how deeply she must be suffering, now that she knew herself to be face to face with his murderer.

She stole a quick glance at him, through her tears. She was deeply penitent for what she had said. It almost seemed to her as if a dual nature was at war within her.

The mention of her brother's name, the recollection of that awful night beside his dead body, of those four years whilst she watched her father's moribund reason slowly wandering towards the grave, seemed to rouse in her a spirit of rebellion, and of evil, which she felt was not entirely of herself.

The woods had become quite silent. It was late afternoon, and they had gradually wandered farther and farther away from pretty sylvan Suresness, towards great, anarchic, deathdealing Paris. In this part of the woods the birds had left their homes; the trees, shorn of their lower branches looked like gaunt spectres, raising melancholy heads towards the relentless, silent sky.

In the distance, from behind the barriers, a couple of miles away, the boom of a gun was heard.

"They are closing the barriers," he said quietly after a long pause. "I am glad I was fortunate enough to meet you."

"It was kind of you to seek for me," she said meekly. "I didn't mean what I said just now ..."

"I pray you, say no more about it. I can so well understand. I only wish ..."

"It would be best I should leave your house," she said gently; "I have so ill repaid your hospitality. Pétronelle and I can easily go back to our lodgings."

"You would break my mother's heart if you left her now," he said, almost roughly. "She has become very fond of you, and knows, just as well as I do, the dangers that would beset you outside my house. My coarse and grimy partisans," he added, with a bitter touch of sarcasm, "have that advantage, that they are loyal to me, and would not harm you while under my roof."

"But you ..." she murmured.

She felt somehow that she had wounded him very deeply, and was half angry with herself for her seeming ingratitude, and yet childishly glad to have suppressed in him that attitude of mentorship, which he was beginning to assume over her.

"You need not fear that my presence will offend you much longer, mademoiselle," he said coldly. "I can quite understand how hateful it must be to you, though I would have wished that you could believe at least in my sincerity."

"Are you going away then?"

"Not out of Paris altogether. I have accepted the post of Governor of the Conciergerie."

"Ah!—where the poor Queen ..."

She checked herself suddenly. Those words would have been called treasonable to the people of France.

Instinctively and furtively, as everyone did in these days, she cast a rapid glance behind her.

"You need not be afraid," he said; "there is no one here but Pétronelle."

"And you."

"Oh! I echo your words. Poor Marie Antoinette!"

"You pity her?"

"How can I help it?"

"But you are of that horrible National Convention, who will try her, condemn her, execute her as they did the King."

"I am of the National Convention. But I will not condemn her, nor be a party to another crime. I go as Governor of the Conciergerie, to help her, if I can."

"But your popularity—your life—if you befriend her?"

"As you say, mademoiselle, my life, if I befriend her," he said simply.

She looked at him with renewed curiosity in her gaze.

How strange were men in these days! Paul Déroulède, the republican, the recognised idol of the lawless people of France, was about to risk his life for the woman he had helped to dethrone.

Pity with him did not end with the rabble of Paris; it had reached Charlotte Corday, though it failed to save her, and now it

23

extended to the poor dispossessed Queen. Somehow, in his face this time, she saw either success or death.

"When do you leave?" she asked.

"To-morrow night."

She said nothing more. Strangely enough, a tinge of melancholy had settled over her spirits. No doubt the proximity of the town was the cause of this. She could already hear the familiar noise of muffled drums, the loud, excited shrieking of the mob, who stood round the gates of Paris, at this time of the evening, waiting to witness some important capture, perhaps that of a hated aristocrat striving to escape from the people's revenge.

They had reached the edge of the wood, and gradually, as she walked, the flowers she had gathered fell unheeded out of her listless hands one by one.

First the blue lupins: their bud-laden heads were heavy and they dropped to the ground, followed by the white marguerites, that lay thick behind her now on the grass like a shroud. The red poppies were the lightest, their thin gummy stalks clung to her hands longer than the rest. At last she let them fall too, singly, like great drops of blood, that glistened as her long white gown swept them aside.

Déroulède was absorbed in his thoughts, and seemed not to heed her. At the barrier, however, he roused himself and took out the passes which alone enabled Juliette and Pétronelle to re-enter the town unchallenged. He himself as Citizen-Deputy could come and go as he wished.

Juliette shuddered as the great gates closed behind her with a heavy clank. It seemed to shut out even the memory of this happy day, which for a brief space had been quite perfect.

She did not know Paris very well, and wondered where lay that gloomy Conciergerie, where a dethroned queen was living her last days, in an agonised memory of the past. But as they crossed the bridge she recognised all round her the massive towers of the great city: Notre Dame, the grateful spire of La Sainte Chapelle, the sombre outline of St. Gervais, and behind her the Louvre with its great history and irreclaimable grandeur. How small her own tragedy seemed in the midst of this great sanguinary drama, the last act of which had not yet even begun. Her own revenge, her oath, her tribulations, what were they in comparison with that great flaming Nemesis which had swept away a throne, that vow of retaliation carried out by thousands against other thousands, that long story of degradation, of regicide, of fratricide, the awesome chapters of which were still being unfolded one by one?

She felt small and petty: ashamed of the pleasure she had felt in the woods, ashamed of her high spirits and light-heartedness,

24

ashamed of that feeling of sudden pity and admiration for the man who had done her and her family so deep an injury, which she was too feeble, too vacillating to avenge.

The majestic outline of the Louvre seemed to frown sarcastically on her weakness, the silent river to mock her and her wavering purpose. The man beside her had wronged her and hers far more deeply than the Bourbons had wronged their people. The people of France were taking their revenge, and God had at the close of this last happy day of her life pointed once more to the means for her great end.

CHAPTER VI

THE SCARLET PIMPERNEL

It was some few hours later. The ladies sat in the drawing-room, silent and anxious.

Soon after supper a visitor had called, and had been closeted with Paul Déroulède in the latter's study for the past two hours.

A tall, somewhat lazy-looking figure, he was sitting at a table face to face with the Citizen-Deputy. On a chair beside him lay a heavy caped coat, covered with the dust and the splashings of a long journey, but he himself was attired in clothes that suggested the most fastidious taste, and the most perfect of tailors; he wore with apparent ease the eccentric fashion of the time, the short-waisted coat of many lapels, the double waistcoat and billows of delicate lace. Unlike Déroulède he was of great height, with fair hair and a somewhat lazy expression in his good-natured blue eyes, and as he spoke, there was just a soupçon of foreign accent in the pronunciation of the French vowels, a certain drawl of o's and a's, that would have betrayed the Britisher to an observant ear.

The two men had been talking earnestly for some time, the tall Englishman was watching his friend keenly, whilst an amused, pleasant smile lingered round the corners of his firm mouth and jaw. Déroulède, restless and enthusiastic, was pacing to and fro.

"But I don't understand now, how you managed to reach Paris, my dear Blakeney!" said Déroulède at last, placing an anxious hand on his friend's shoulder. "The government has not forgotten The Scarlet Pimpernel."

"La! I took care of that!" responded Blakeney with his short, pleasant laugh. "I sent Tinville my autograph this morning."

"You are mad, Blakeney!"

"Not altogether, my friend. My faith! 'twas not only foolhardiness caused me to grant that devilish prosecutor another sight of my scarlet device. I knew what you maniacs would be after, so I came across in the Daydream, just to see if I couldn't get my share of the fun."

"Fun, you call it?" queried the other bitterly.

"Nay! what would you have me call it? A mad, insane, senseless tragedy, with but one issue?—the guillotine for you all."

"Then why did you come?"

"To—What shall I say, my friend?" rejoined Sir Percy

26

Blakeney, with that inimitable drawl of his. "To give your demmed government something else to think about, whilst you are all busy running your heads into a noose."

"What makes you think we are doing that?"

"Three things, my friend—may I offer you a pinch of snuff—No?—Ah well!..." And with the graceful gesture of an accomplished dandy, Sir Percy flicked off a grain of dust from his immaculate Mechlin ruffles.

"Three things," he continued quietly; "an imprisoned Queen, about to be tried for her life, the temperament of a Frenchman—some of them— and the idiocy of mankind generally. These three things make me think that a certain section of hot-headed Republicans with yourself, my dear Déroulède, en tête, are about to attempt the most stupid, senseless, purposeless thing that was ever concocted by the excitable brain of a demmed Frenchman."

Déroulède smiled.

"Does it not seem amusing to you, Blakeney, that you should sit there and condemn anyone for planning mad, insane, senseless things."

"La! I'll not sit, I'll stand!" rejoined Blakeney with a laugh, as he drew himself up to his full height, and stretched his long, lazy limbs. "And now let me tell you, friend, that my League of The Scarlet Pimpernel never attempted the impossible, and to try and drag the Queen out of the clutches of these murderous rascals now, is attempting the unattainable."

"And yet we mean to try."

"I know it. I guessed it, that is why I came: that is also why I sent a pleasant little note to the Committee of Public Safety, signed with the device they know so well: The Scarlet Pimpernel."

"Well?"

"Well! the result is obvious. Robespierre, Danton, Tinville, Merlin, and the whole of the demmed murderous crowd, will be busy looking after me—a needle in a haystack. They'll put the abortive attempt down to me, and you may—ma foi! I only suggest that you may escape safely out of France—in the Daydream, and with the help of your humble servant."

"But in the meanwhile they'll discover you, and they'll not let you escape a second time."

"My friend! if a terrier were to lose his temper, he never would run a rat to earth. Now your Revolutionary Government has lost its temper with me, ever since I slipped through Chauvelin's fingers; they are blind with their own fury, whilst I am perfectly happy and cool as a cucumber. My life has become valuable to me, my friend. There is someone over the water now who weeps when I don't

27

return—No! no! never fear—they'll not get The Scarlet Pimpernel this journey ..."

He laughed, a gay, pleasant laugh, and his strong, firm face seemed to soften at thought of the beautiful wife, over in England, who was waiting anxiously for his safe return.

"And yet you'll not help us to rescue the Queen?" rejoined Déroulède, with some bitterness.

"By every means in my power," replied Blakeney, "save the insane. But I will help to get you all out of the demmed hole, when you have failed."

"We'll not fail," asserted the other hotly.

Sir Percy Blakeney went close up to his friend and placed his long, slender hand, with a touch of almost womanly tenderness upon the latter's shoulder.

"Will you tell me your plans?"

In a moment Déroulède was all fire and enthusiasm.

"There are not many of us in it," he began, "although half France will be in sympathy with us. We have plenty of money, of course, and also the necessary disguise for the royal lady."

"Yes?"

"I, in the meanwhile, have asked for and obtained the post of Governor of the Conciergerie; I go into my new quarters to-morrow. In the meanwhile, I am making arrangements for my mother and—and those dependent upon me to quit France immediately."

Blakeney had perceived the slight hesitation when Déroulède mentioned those dependent upon him. He looked scrutinisingly at his friend, who continued quickly:

"I am still very popular among the people. My family can go about unmolested. I must get them out of France, however, in case—in case ..."

"Of course," rejoined the other simply.

"As soon as I am assured that they are safe, my friends and I can prosecute our plans. You see the trial of the Queen has not yet been decided on, but I know that it is in the air. We hope to get her away, disguised in one of the uniforms of the National Guard. As you know, it will be my duty to make the final round every evening in the prison, and to see that everything is safe for the night. Two fellows watch all night, in the room next to that occupied by the Queen. Usually they drink and play cards all night long. I want an opportunity to drug their brandy, and thus to render them more loutish and idiotic than usual; then for a blow on the head that will make them senseless. It should be easy, for I have a strong fist, and after that ..."

"Well? After that, friend?" rejoined Sir Percy earnestly, "after that? Shall I fill in the details of the picture?—the guard twenty-five strong outside the Conciergerie, how will you pass them?"

"I as the Governor, followed by one of my guards ..."

"To go whither?"

"I have the right to come and go as I please."

"I' faith! so you have, but 'one of your guards'—eh? Wrapped to the eyes in a long mantle to hide the female figure beneath. I have been in Paris but a few hours, and yet already I have realised that there is not one demmed citizen within its walls, who does not at this moment suspect some other demmed citizen of conniving at the Queen's escape. Even the sparrows on the house-tops are objects of suspicion. No figure wrapped in a mantle will from this day forth leave Paris unchallenged."

"But you yourself, friend?" suggested Déroulède. "You think you can quit Paris unrecognised—then why not the Queen?"

"Because she is a woman, and has been a queen. She has nerves, poor soul, and weaknesses of body and of mind now. Alas for her! Alas for France! who wreaks such idle vengeance on so poor an enemy? Can you take hold of Marie Antoinette by the shoulders, shove her into the bottom of a cart and pile sacks of potatoes on the top of her? I did that to the Comtesse de Tournai and her daughter, as stiff-necked a pair of French aristocrats as ever deserved the guillotine for their insane prejudices. But can you do it to Marie Antoinette? She'd rebuke you publicly, and betray herself and you in a flash, sooner than submit to a loss of dignity."

"But would you leave her to her fate?"

"Ah! there's the trouble, friend. Do you think you need appeal to the sense of chivalry of my league? We are still twenty strong, and heart and soul in sympathy with your mad schemes. The poor, poor Queen! But you are bound to fail, and then who will help you all, if we too are put out of the way?"

"We should succeed if you helped us. At one time you used proudly to say: 'The League of The Scarlet Pimpernel has never failed.'"

"Because it attempted nothing which it could not accomplish. But, la! since you put me on my mettle—Demm it all! I'll have to think about it!"

And he laughed that funny, somewhat inane laugh of his, which had deceived the clever men of two countries as to his real personality.

Déroulède went up to the heavy oak desk which occupied a conspicuous place in the centre of one of the walls. He unlocked it and drew forth a bundle of papers.

29

"Will you look through these?" he asked, handing them to Sir Percy Blakeney.

"What are they?"

"Different schemes I have drawn up, in case my original plan should not succeed."

"Burn them, my friend," said Blakeney laconically. "Have you not yet learned the lesson of never putting your hand to paper?"

"I can't burn these. You see, I shall not be able to have long conversations with Marie Antoinette. I must give her my suggestions in writing, that she may study them and not fail me, through lack of knowledge of her part."

"Better that than papers in these times, my friend: these papers, if found, would send you, untried, to the guillotine."

"I am careful, and, at present, quite beyond suspicion. Moreover, among the papers is a complete collection of passports, suitable for any character the Queen and her attendant may be forced to assume. It has taken me some months to collect them, so as not to arouse suspicion; I gradually got them together, on one pretence or another: now I am ready for any eventuality ..."

He suddenly paused. A look in his friend's face had given him a swift warning.

He turned, and there in the doorway, holding back the heavy portière, stood Juliette, graceful, smiling, a little pale, this no doubt owing to the flickering light of the unsnuffed candles.

So young and girlish did she look in her soft, white muslin frock that at sight of her the tension in Déroulède's face seemed to relax. Instinctively he had thrown the papers back into the desk, but his look had softened, from the fire of obstinate energy to that of inexpressible tenderness.

Blakeney was quietly watching the young girl as she stood in the doorway, a little bashful and undecided.

"Madame Déroulède sent me," she said hesitatingly, "she says the hour is getting late and she is very anxious. M. Déroulède, would you come and reassure her?"

"In a moment, mademoiselle," he replied lightly, "my friend and I have just finished our talk. May I have the honour to present him?—Sir Percy Blakeney, a traveller from England. Blakeney, this is Mademoiselle Juliette de Marny, my mother's guest."

CHAPTER VII

A WARNING

Sir Percy bowed very low, with all the graceful flourish and elaborate gesture the eccentric customs of the time demanded.

He had not said a word, since the first exclamation of warning, with which he had drawn his friend's attention to the young girl in the doorway.

Noiselessly, as she had come, Juliette glided out of the room again, leaving behind her an atmosphere of wild flowers, of the bouquet she had gathered, then scattered in the woods.

There was silence in the room for awhile. Déroulède was locking up his desk and slipping the keys into his pocket.

"Shall we join my mother for a moment, Blakeney?" he said, moving towards the door.

"I shall be proud to pay my respects," replied Sir Percy; "but before we close the subject, I think I'll change my mind about those papers. If I am to be of service to you I think I had best look through them, and give you my opinion of your schemes."

Déroulède looked at him keenly for a moment.

"Certainly," he said at last, going up to his desk. "I'll stay with you whilst you read them through."

"La! not to-night, my friend," said Sir Percy lightly; "the hour is late, and madame is waiting for us. They'll be quite safe with me, and you'll entrust them to my care."

Déroulède seemed to hesitate. Blakeney had spoken in his usual airy manner, and was even now busy readjusting the set of his perfectly-tailored coat.

"Perhaps you cannot quite trust me?" laughed Sir Percy gaily. "I seemed too lukewarm just now."

"No; it's not that, Blakeney!" said Déroulède quietly at last. "There is no mistrust in me, all the mistrust is on your side."

"Faith!—" began Sir Percy.

"Nay! do not explain. I understand and appreciate your friendship, but I should like to convince you how unjust is your mistrust of one of God's purest angels, that ever walked the earth."

"Oho! that's it, is it, friend Déroulède? Methought you had foresworn the sex altogether, and now you are in love."

"Madly, blindly, stupidly in love, my friend," said Déroulède with a sigh. "Hopelessly, I fear me!"

31

"Why hopelessly?"

"She is the daughter of the late Duc de Marny, one of the oldest names in France; a Royalist to the backbone ..."

"Hence your overwhelming sympathy for the Queen!"

"Nay! you wrong me there, friend. I'd have tried to save the Queen, even if I had never learned to love Juliette. But you see now how unjust were your suspicions."

"Had I any?"

"Don't deny it. You were loud in urging me to burn those papers a moment ago. You called them useless and dangerous and now ..."

"I still think them useless and dangerous, and by reading them would wish to confirm my opinion and give weight to my arguments."

"If I were to part from them now I would seem to be mistrusting her."

"You are a mad idealist, my dear Déroulède!"

"How can I help it? I have lived under the same roof with her for three weeks now. I have begun to understand what a saint is like."

"And 'twill be when you understand that your idol has feet of clay that you'll learn the real lesson of love," said Blakeney earnestly.

"Is it love to worship a saint in heaven, whom you dare not touch, who hovers above you like a cloud, which floats away from you even as you gaze? To love is to feel one being in the world at one with us, our equal in sin as well as in virtue. To love, for us men, is to clasp one woman with our arms, feeling that she lives and breathes just as we do, suffers as we do, thinks with us, loves with us, and, above all, sins with us. Your mock saint who stands in a niche is not a woman if she have not suffered, still less a woman if she have not sinned. Fall at the feet of your idol an you wish, but drag her down to your level after that—the only level she should ever reach, that of your heart."

Who shall render faithfully a true account of the magnetism which poured forth from this remarkable man as he spoke: this well-dressed, foppish apostle of the greatest love that man has ever known. And as he spoke the whole story of his own great, true love for the woman who once had so deeply wronged him seemed to stand clearly written in the strong, lazy, good-humoured, kindly face glowing with tenderness for her.

Déroulède felt this magnetism, and therefore did not resent the implied suggestion, anent the saint whom he was still content to worship.

A dreamer and an idealist, his mind held spellbound by the great social problems which were causing the upheaval of a whole country, he had not yet had the time to learn the sweet lesson which Nature teaches to her elect—the lesson of a great, a true, human and passionate love. To him, at present, Juliette represented the perfect embodiment of his most idealistic dreams. She stood in his mind so far above him that if she proved unattainable, he would scarce have suffered. It was such a foregone conclusion.

Blakeney's words were the first to stir in his heart a desire for something beyond that quasi-mediaeval worship, something weaker and yet infinitely stronger, something more earthy and yet almost divine.

"And now, shall we join the ladies?" said Blakeney after a long pause, during which the mental workings of his alert brain were almost visible, in the earnest look which he cast at his friend. "You shall keep the papers in your desk, give them into the keeping of your saint, trust her all in all rather than not at all, and if the time should come that your heaven-enthroned ideal fall somewhat heavily to earth, then give me the privilege of being a witness to your happiness."

"You are still mistrustful, Blakeney," said Déroulède lightly. "If you say much more I'll give these papers into Mademoiselle Marny's keeping until to-morrow."

CHAPTER VIII

ANNE MIE

That night, when Blakeney, wrapped in his cloak, was walking down the Rue Ecole de Médecine towards his own lodgings, he suddenly felt a timid hand upon his sleeve.

Anne Mie stood beside him, her pale, melancholy face peeping up at the tall Englishman, through the folds of a dark hood closely tied under her chin.

"Monsieur," she said timidly, "do not think me very presumptuous. I— I would wish to have five minutes' talk with you—may I?"

He looked down with great kindness at the quaint, wizened little figure, and the strong face softened at the sight of the poor, deformed shoulder, the hard, pinched look of the young mouth, the general look of pathetic helplessness which appeals so strongly to the chivalrous.

"Indeed, mademoiselle," he said gently, "you make me very proud; and I can serve you in any way, I pray you command me. But," he added, seeing Anne Mie's somewhat scared look, "this street is scarce fit for private conversation. Shall we try and find a better spot?"

Paris had not yet gone to bed. In these times it was really safest to be out in the open streets. There, everybody was more busy, more on the move, on the lookout for suspected houses, leaving the wanderer alone.

Blakeney led Anne Mie towards the Luxembourg Gardens, the great devastated pleasure-ground of the ci-devant tyrants of the people. The beautiful Anne of Austria, and the Medici before her, Louis XIII, and his gallant musketeers—all have given place to the great cannon-forging industry of this besieged Republic. France, attacked on every side, is forcing her sons to defend her: persecuted, martyrised, done to death by her, she is still their Mother: La Patrie, who needs their arms against the foreign foe. England is threatening the north, Prussia and Austria the east. Admiral Hood's flag is flying on Toulon Arsenal.

The siege of the Republic!

And the Republic is fighting for dear life. The Tuileries and Luxembourg Gardens are transformed into a township of gigantic smithies; and Anne Mie, with scared eyes, and clinging to

34

Blakeney's arm, cast furtive, terrified glances at the huge furnaces and the begrimed, darkly scowling faces of the workers within.

"The people of France in arms against tyranny!" Great placards, bearing these inspiriting words, are affixed to gallows-shaped posts, and flutter in the evening breeze, rendered scorching by the heat of the furnaces all around.

Farther on, a group of older men, squatting on the ground, are busy making tents, and some women—the same Megaeras who daily shriek round the guillotine—are plying their needles and scissors for the purpose of making clothes for the soldiers.

The soldiers are the entire able-bodied male population of France.

"The people of France in arms against tyranny!"

That is their sign, their trade-mark; one of these placards, fitfully illumined by a torch of resin, towers above a group of children busy tearing up scraps of old linen—their mothers', their sisters' linen —in order to make lint for the wounded.

Loud curses and suppressed mutterings fill the smoke-laden air.

The people of France, in arms against tyranny, is bending its broad back before the most cruel, the most absolute and brutish slave-driving ever exercised over mankind.

Not even mediaeval Christianity has ever dared such wholesale enforcements of its doctrines, as this constitution of Liberty and Fraternity.

Merlin's "Law of the Suspect" has just been formulated. From now onward each and every citizen of France must watch his words, his looks, his gestures, lest they be suspect. Of what—of treason to the Republic, to the people? Nay, worse! lest they be suspect of being suspect to the great era of Liberty.

Therefore in the smithies and among the groups of tent-makers a moment's negligence, a careless attention to the work, might lead to a brief trial on the morrow and the inevitable guillotine. Negligence is treason to the higher interests of the Republic.

Blakeney dragged Anne Mie away from the sight. These roaring furnaces frightened her; he took her down the Place St Michel, towards the river. It was quieter here.

"What dreadful people they have become," she said, shuddering; "even I can remember how different they used to be."

The houses on the banks of the river were mostly converted into hospitals, preparatory for the great siege. Some hundred mètres lower down, the new children's hospital, endowed by

35

Citizen-Deputy Déroulède, loomed, white, clean, and comfortable-looking, amidst its more squalid fellows.

"I think it would be best not to sit down," suggested Blakeney, "and wiser for you to throw your hood away from your face."

He seemed to have no fears for himself; many had said that he bore a charmed life; and yet ever since Admiral Hood had planted his flag on Toulon Arsenal, the English were more feared than ever, and The Scarlet Pimpernel more hated than most.

"You wished to speak to me about Paul Déroulède," he said kindly, seeing that the young girl was making desperate efforts to say what lay on her mind. "He is my friend, you know."

"Yes; that is why I wished to ask you a question," she replied.

"What is it?"

"Who is Juliette de Marny, and why did she seek an entrance into Paul's house?"

"Did she seek it, then?"

"Yes; I saw the scene from the balcony. At the time it did not strike me as a farce. I merely thought that she had been stupid and foolhardy. But since then I have reflected. She provoked the mob of the street, wilfully, just at the very moment when she reached M. Déroulède's door. She meant to appeal to his chivalry, and called for help, well knowing that he would respond."

She spoke rapidly and excitedly now, throwing off all shyness and reserve. Blakeney was forced to check her vehemence, which might have been thought "suspicious" by some idle citizen unpleasantly inclined.

"Well? And now?" he asked, for the young girl had paused, as if ashamed of her excitement.

"And now she stays in the house, on and on, day after day," continued Anne Mie, speaking more quietly, though with no less intensity. "Why does she not go? She is not safe in France. She belongs to the most hated of all the classes—the idle, rich aristocrats of the old régime. Paul has several times suggested plans for her emigration to England. Madame Déroulède, who is an angel, loves her, and would not like to part from her, but it would be obviously wiser for her to go, and yet she stays. Why?"

"Presumably because ..."

"Because she is in love with Paul?" interrupted Anne Mie vehemently. "No, no; she does not love him—at least—Oh! sometimes I don't know. Her eyes light up when he comes, and she is listless when he goes. She always spends a longer time over her toilet, when we expect him home to dinner," she added, with a touch of naïve femininity. "But— if it be love, then that love is strange and unwomanly; it is a love that will not be for his good ..."

36

"Why should you think that?"

"I don't know," said the girl simply. "Isn't it an instinct?"

"Not a very unerring one in this case, I fear."

"Why?"

"Because your own love for Paul Déroulède has blinded you— Ah! you must pardon me, mademoiselle; you sought this conversation and not I, and I fear me I have wounded you. Yet I would wish you to know how deep is my sympathy with you, and how great my desire to render you a service if I could."

"I was about to ask a service of you, monsieur."

"Then command me, I beg of you."

"You are Paul's friend—persuade him that that woman in his house is a standing danger to his life and liberty."

"He would not listen to me."

"Oh! a man always listens to another."

"Except on one subject—the woman he loves."

He had said the last words very gently but very firmly. He was deeply, tenderly sorry for the poor, deformed, fragile girl, doomed to be a witness of that most heartrending of human tragedies, the passing away of her own scarce-hoped-for happiness. But he felt that at this moment the kindest act would be one of complete truth. He knew that Paul Déroulède's heart was completely given to Juliette de Marny; he too, like Anne Mie, instinctively mistrusted the beautiful girl and her strange, silent ways, but, unlike the poor hunchback, he knew that no sin which Juliette might commit would henceforth tear her from out the heart of his friend; that if, indeed, she turned out to be false, or even treacherous, she would, nevertheless, still hold a place in Déroulède's very soul, which no one else would ever fill.

"You think he loves her?" asked Anne Mie at last.

"I am sure of it."

"And she?"

"Ah! I do not know. I would trust your instinct—a woman's— sooner than my own."

"She is false, I tell you, and is hatching treason against Paul."

"Then all we can do is to wait."

"Wait?"

"And watch carefully, earnestly, all the time. There! shall I pledge you my word that Déroulède shall come to no harm?"

"Pledge me your word that you'll part him from that woman."

"Nay; that is beyond my power. A man like Paul Déroulède only loves once in life, but when he does, it is for always."

Once more she was silent, pressing her lips closely together, as if afraid of what she might say.

He saw that she was bitterly disappointed, and sought for a means of tempering the cruelty of the blow.

"It will be your task to watch over Paul," he said; "with your friendship to guard and protect him, we need have no fear for his safety, I think."

"I will watch," she replied quietly.

Gradually he had led her steps back towards the Rue Ecole de Médecine.

A great melancholy had fallen over his bold, adventurous spirit. How full of tragedies was this great city, in the last throes of its insane and cruel struggle for an unattainable goal. And yet, despite its guillotine and mock trials, its tyrannical laws and overfilled prisons, its very sorrows paled before the dead, dull misery of this deformed girl's heart.

A wild exaltation, a fever of enthusiasm lent glamour to the scenes which were daily enacted on the Place de la Revolution, turning the final acts of the tragedies into glaring, lurid melodrama, almost unreal in its poignant appeal to the sensibilities.

But here there was only this dead, dull misery, an aching heart, a poor, fragile creature in the throes of an agonised struggle for a fast-disappearing happiness.

Anne Mie hardly knew now what she had hoped, when she sought this interview with Sir Percy Blakeney. Drowning in a sea of hopelessness, she had clutched at what might prove a chance of safety. Her reason told her that Paul's friend was right. Déroulède was a man who would love but once in his life. He had never loved— for he had too much pitied—poor, pathetic little Anne Mie.

Nay; why should we say that love and pity are akin?

Love, the great, the strong, the conquering god—Love that subdues a world, and rides roughshod over principle, virtue, tradition, over home, kindred, and religion—what cares he for the easy conquest of the pathetic being, who appeals to his sympathy?

Love means equality—the same height of heroism or of sin. When Love stoops to pity, he has ceased to soar in the boundless space, that rarefied atmosphere wherein man feels himself made at last truly in the image of God.

CHAPTER IX

JEALOUSY

At the door of her home Blakeney parted from Anne Mie, with all the courtesy with which he would have bade adieu to the greatest lady in his own land.

Anne Mie let herself into the house with her own latch-key. She closed the heavy door noiselessly, then glided upstairs like a quaint little ghost.

But on the landing above she met Paul Déroulède.

He had just come out of his room, and was still fully dressed.

"Anne Mie!" he said, with such an obvious cry of pleasure, that the young girl, with beating heart, paused a moment on the top of the stairs, as if hoping to hear that cry again, feeling that indeed he was glad to see her, had been uneasy because of her long absence.

"Have I made you anxious?" she asked at last.

"Anxious!" he exclaimed. "Little one, I have hardly lived this last hour, since I realised that you had gone out so late as this, and all alone."

"How did you know?"

"Mademoiselle de Marny knocked at my door an hour ago. She had gone to your room to see you, and, not finding you there, she searched the house for you, and finally, in her anxiety, came to me. We did not dare to tell my mother. I won't ask you where you have been, Anne Mie, but another time, remember, little one, that the streets of Paris are not safe, and that those who love you suffer deeply, when they know you to be in peril."

"Those who love me!" murmured the girl under her breath.

"Could you not have asked me to come with you?"

"No; I wanted to be alone. The streets were quite safe, and—I wanted to speak with Sir Percy Blakeney."

"With Blakeney?" he exclaimed in boundless astonishment. "Why, what in the world did you want to say him?"

The girl, so unaccustomed to lying, had blurted out the truth, almost against her will.

"I thought he could help me, as I was much perturbed and restless."

"You went to him sooner than to me?" said Déroulède in a

tone of gentle reproach, and still puzzled at this extraordinary action on the part of the girl, usually so shy and reserved.

"My anxiety was about you, and you would have mocked me for it."

"Indeed, I should never mock you, Anne Mie. But why should you be anxious about me?"

"Because I see you wandering blindly on the brink of a great danger, and because I see you confiding in those, whom you had best mistrust."

He frowned a little, and bit his lip to check the rough word that was on the tip of his tongue.

"Is Sir Percy Blakeney one of those whom I had best mistrust?" he said lightly.

"No," she answered curtly.

"Then, dear, there is no cause for unrest. He is the only one of my friends whom you have not known intimately. All those who are round me now, you know that you can trust and that you can love," he added earnestly and significantly.

He took her hand; it was trembling with obvious suppressed agitation. She knew that he had guessed what was passing in her mind, and now was deeply ashamed of what she had done. She had been tortured with jealousy for the past three weeks, but at least she had suffered quite alone: no one had been allowed to touch that wound, which more often than not, excites derision rather than pity. Now, by her own actions, two men knew her secret. Both were kind and sympathetic; but Déroulède resented her imputations, and Blakeney had been unable to help her.

A wave of morbid introspection swept over her soul. She realised in a moment how petty and base had been her thoughts and how purposeless her actions. She would have given her life at this moment to eradicate from Déroulède's mind the knowledge of her own jealousy; she hoped that at least he had not guessed her love.

She tried to read his thoughts, but in the dark passage, only dimly lighted by the candles in Déroulède's room beyond, she could not see the expression of his face, but the hand which held hers was warm and tender. She felt herself pitied, and blushed at the thought. With a hasty good-night she fled down the passage, and locked herself in her room, alone with her own thoughts at last.

40

CHAPTER X

DENUNCIATION

But what of Juliette?

What of this wild, passionate, romantic creature tortured by a Titanic conflict? She, but a girl, scarcely yet a woman, torn by the greatest antagonistic powers that ever fought for a human soul. On the one side duty, tradition, her dead brother, her father—above all, her religion and the oath she had sworn before God; on the other justice and honour, a case of right and wrong, honesty and pity.

How she fought with these powers now!

She fought with them, struggled with them on her knees. She tried to crush memory, tried to forget that awful midnight scene ten years ago, her brother's dead body, her father's avenging hand holding her own, as he begged her to do that, which he was too feeble, too old to accomplish.

His words rang in her ears from across that long vista of the past.

"Before the face of Almighty God, who sees and hears me, I swear ..."

And she had repeated those words loudly and of her own free will, with her hand resting on her brother's breast, and God Himself looking down upon her, for she had called upon Him to listen.

"I swear that I will seek out Paul Déroulède, and in any manner which God may dictate to me encompass his death, his ruin, or dishonour in revenge for my brother's death. May my brother's soul remain in torment until the final Judgment Day if I should break my oath, but may it rest in eternal peace, the day on which his death is fitly avenged."

Almost it seemed to her as if father and brother were standing by her side, as she knelt and prayed.—Oh! how she prayed!

In many ways she was only a child. All her years had been passed in confinement, either beside her dying father or, later, between the four walls of the Ursuline Convent. And during those years her soul had been fed on a contemplative, ecstatic religion, a kind of sanctified superstition, which she would have deemed sacrilege to combat.

Her first step into womanhood was taken with that oath upon her lips; since then, with a stoical sense of duty, she had lashed

41

herself into a daily, hourly remembrance of the great mission imposed upon her.

To have neglected it would have been, to her, equal to denying God.

She had but vague ideas of the doctrinal side of religion. Purgatory was to her merely a word, but a word representing a real spiritual state—one of expectancy, of restlessness, of sorrow. And vaguely, yet determinedly, she believed that her brother's soul suffered, because she had been too weak to fulfil her oath.

The Church had not come to her rescue. The ministers of her religion were scattered to the four corners of besieged, agonising France. She had no one to help her, no one to comfort her. That very peaceful, contemplative life she had led in the convent, only served to enhance her feeling of the solemnity of her mission.

It was true, it was inevitable, because it was so hard.

To the few who, throughout those troublous times, had kept a feeling of veneration for their religion, this religion had become one of abnegation and martyrdom.

A spirit of uncompromising Jansenism seemed to call forth sacrifices and renunciation, whereas the happy-go-lucky Catholicism of the past century had only suggested an easy, flowered path, to a comfortable, well-upholstered heaven.

The harder the task seemed which was set before her, the more real it became to Juliette. God, she firmly believed, had at last, after ten years, shown her the way to wreak vengeance upon her brother's murderer. He had brought her to this house, caused her to see and hear part of the conversation between Blakeney and Déroulède, and this at the moment of all others, when even the semblance of a conspiracy against the Republic would bring the one inevitable result in its train: disgrace first, the hasty mock trial, the hall of justice, and the guillotine.

She tried not to hate Déroulède. She wished to judge him coldly and impartially, or rather to indict him before the throne of God, and to punish him for the crime he had committed ten years ago. Her personal feelings must remain out of the question.

Had Charlotte Corday considered her own sensibilities, when with her own hand she put an end to Marat?

Juliette remained on her knees for hours. She heard Anne Mie come home, and Déroulède's voice of welcome on the landing. This was perhaps the most bitter moment of this awful soul conflict, for it brought to her mind the remembrance of those others who would suffer too, and who were innocent—Madame Déroulède and poor, crippled Anne Mie. They had done no wrong, and yet how heavily would they be punished!

And then the saner judgment, the human, material code of ethics gained for a while the upper hand. Juliette would rise from her knees, dry her eyes, prepare quietly to go to bed, and to forget all about the awful, relentless Fate which dragged her to the fulfilment of its will, and then sink back, broken-hearted, murmuring impassioned prayers for forgiveness to her father, her brother, her God.

The soul was young and ardent, and it fought for abnegation, martyrdom, and stern duty; the body was childlike, and it fought for peace, contentment, and quiet reason.

The rational body was conquered by the passionate, powerful soul.

Blame not the child, for in herself she was innocent. She was but another of the many victims of this cruel, mad, hysterical time, that spirit of relentless tyranny, forcing its doctrines upon the weak.

With the first break of dawn Juliette at last finally rose from her knees, bathed her burning eyes and head, tidied her hair and dress, then she sat down at the table, and began to write.

She was a transformed being now, no longer a child, essentially a woman—a Joan of Arc with a mission, a Charlotte Corday going to martyrdom, a human, suffering, erring soul, committing a great crime for the sake of an idea.

She wrote out carefully and with a steady hand the denunciation of Citizen-Deputy Déroulède which has become an historical document, and is preserved in the chronicles of France.

You have all seen it at the Musée Carnavalet in its glass case, its yellow paper and faded ink revealing nothing of the soul conflict of which it was the culminating victory. The cramped, somewhat schoolgirlish writing is the mute, pathetic witness of one of the saddest tragedies, that era of sorrow and crime has ever known:

> *To the Representatives of the People now sitting in Assembly at the National Convention*
> You trust and believe in the Representative of the people: Citizen-Deputy Paul Déroulède. He is false, and a traitor to the Republic. He is planning, and hopes to effect, the release of ci-devant Marie Antoinette, widow of the traitor Louis Capet. Haste! ye representatives of the people! proofs of his assertion, papers and plans, are still in the house of the Citizen-Deputy Déroulède. This statement is made by one who knows.
> I. The 23rd Fructidor.

When her letter was written she read it through carefully, made the one or two little corrections, which are still visible in the

43

document, then folded her missive, hid it within the folds of her kerchief, and, wrapping a dark cloak and hood round her, she slipped noiselessly out of her room.

The house was all quiet and still. She shuddered a little as the cool morning air fanned her hot cheeks: it seemed like the breath of ghosts.

She ran quickly down the stairs, and as rapidly as she could, pushed back the heavy bolts of the front door, and slipped out into the street.

Already the city was beginning to stir. There was no time for sleep, when so much had to be done for the safety of the threatened Republic. As Juliette turned her steps towards the river, she met the crowd of workmen, whom France was employing for her defence.

Behind her, in the Luxembourg Gardens, and all along the opposite bank of the river, the furnaces were already ablaze, and the smiths at work forging the guns.

At every step now Juliette came across the great placards, pinned to the tall gallows-shaped posts, which proclaim to every passing citizen, that the people of France are up and in arms.

Right across the Place de l'Institut a procession of market carts, laden with vegetables and a little fruit, wends its way slowly towards the centre of the town. They each carry tiny tricolour flags, with a Pike and Cap of Liberty surmounting the flagstaff.

They are good patriots the market-gardeners, who come in daily to feed the starving mob of Paris, with the few handfuls of watery potatoes, and miserable, vermin-eaten cabbages, which that fraternal Revolution still allows them to grow without hindrance.

Everyone seems busy with their work this early in the morning: the business of killing does not begin until later in the day.

For the moment Juliette can get along quite unmolested: the women and children mostly hurrying on towards the vast encampments in the Tuileries, where lint, and bandages, and coats for the soldiers are manufactured all the day.

The walls of all the houses bear the great patriotic device: "Liberté, Egalité, Fraternité, sinon La Mort "; others are more political in their proclamation: "La République une et indivisible ."

But on the walls of the Louvre, of the great palace of whilom kings, where the Roi Soleil held his Court, and flirted with the prettiest women in France, there the new and great Republic has affixed its final mandate.

A great poster glued to the wall bears the words: "La Loi concernan les Suspects ." Below the poster is a huge wooden box with a slit at the top.

44

This is the latest invention for securing the safety of this one and indivisible Republic.

Henceforth everyone becomes a traitor at one word of denunciation from an idler or an enemy, and, as in the most tyrannical days of the Spanish Inquisition one-half of the nation was set to spy upon the other, that wooden box, with its slit, is put there ready to receive denunciations from one hand against another.

Had Juliette paused but for the fraction of a second, had she stopped to read the placard setting forth this odious law, had she only reflected, then she would even now have turned back, and fled from that gruesome box of infamies, as she would from a dangerous and noisome reptile or from the pestilence.

But her long vigil, her prayers, her ecstatic visions of heroic martyrs had now completely numbed her faculties. Her vitality, her sensibilities were gone: she had become an automaton gliding to her doom, without a thought or a tremor.

She drew the letter from her bosom, and with a steady hand dropped it into the box. The irreclaimable had now occurred. Nothing she could henceforth say or do, no prayers or agonised vigils, no miracles even, could undo her action or save Paul Déroulède from trial and guillotine.

One or two groups of people hurrying to their work had seen her drop the letter into the box. A couple of small children paused, finger in mouth, gazing at her with inane curiosity; one woman uttered a coarse jest, all of them shrugged their shoulders, and passed on, on their way. Those who habitually crossed this spot were used to such sights.

That wooden box, with its mouthlike slit was like an insatiable monster that was constantly fed, yet was still gaping for more.

Having done the deed Juliette turned, and as rapidly as she had come, so she went back to her temporary home.

A home no more now; she must leave it at once, to-day if possible. This much she knew, that she no longer could touch the bread of the man she had betrayed. She would not appear at breakfast, she could plead a headache, and in the afternoon Pétronelle should pack her things.

She turned into a little shop close by, and asked for a glass of milk and a bit of bread. The woman who served her eyed her with some curiosity, for Juliette just now looked almost out of her mind.

She had not yet begun to think, and she had ceased to suffer.

Both would come presently, and with them the memory of this last irretrievable hour and a just estimate of what she had done.

45

CHAPTER XI

"VENGEANCE IS MINE"

The pretence of a headache enabled Juliette to keep in her room the greater part of the day. She would have liked to shut herself out from the entire world during those hours which she spent face to face with her own thoughts and her own sufferings.

The sight of Anne Mie's pathetic little face as she brought her food and delicacies and various little comforts, was positive torture to the poor, harrowed soul.

At every sound in the great, silent house she started up, quivering with apprehension and horror. Had the sword of Damocles, which she herself had suspended, already fallen over the heads of those who had shown her nothing but kindness?

She could not think of Madame Déroulède or of Anne Mie without the most agonising, the most torturing shame.

And what of him—the man she had so remorselessly, so ruthlessly betrayed to a tribunal which would know no mercy?

Juliette dared not think of him.

She had never tried to analyse her feelings with regard to him. At the time of Charlotte Corday's trial, when his sonorous voice rang out in its pathetic appeal for the misguided woman, Juliette had given him ungrudging admiration. She remembered now how strongly his magnetic personality had roused in her a feeling of enthusiasm for the poor girl, who had come from the depths of her quiet provincial home, in order to accomplish the horrible deed which would immortalise her name through all the ages to come, and cause her countrymen to proclaim her "greater than Brutus."

Déroulède was pleading for the life of that woman, and it was his very appeal which had aroused Juliette's dormant energy, for the cause which her dead father had enjoined her not to forget. It was Déroulède again whom she had seen but a few weeks ago, standing alone before the mob who would have torn her to pieces, haranguing them on her behalf, speaking to them with that quiet, strong voice of his, ruling them with the rule of love and pity, and turning their wrath to gentleness.

Did she hate him, then?

Surely, surely she hated him for having thrust himself into her life, for having caused her brother's death and covered her father's declining years with sorrow. And, above all, she hated him—indeed,

indeed it was hate!—for being the cause of this most hideous action of her life: an action to which she had been driven against her will, one of basest ingratitude and treachery, foreign to every sentiment within her heart, cowardly, abject, the unconscious outcome of this strange magnetism which emanated from him and had cast a spell over her, transforming her individuality and will power, and making of her an unconscious and automatic instrument of Fate.

She would not speak of God's finger again: it was Fate—pagan, devilish Fate!—the weird, shrivelled women who sit and spin their interminable thread. They had decreed; and Juliette, unable to fight, blind and broken by the conflict, had succumbed to the Megaeras and their relentless wheel.

At length silence and loneliness became unendurable. She called Pétronelle, and ordered her to pack her boxes.

"We leave for England to-day", she said curtly.

"For England?" gasped the worthy old soul, who was feeling very happy and comfortable in this hospitable house, and was loth to leave it. "So soon?"

"Why, yes; we had talked of it for some time. We cannot remain here always. My cousins De Crécy are there, and my aunt De Coudremont. We shall be among friends, Pétronelle, if we ever get there."

"If we ever get there!" sighed poor Pétronelle; "we have but very little money, ma chérie, and no passports. Have you thought of asking M. Déroulède for them?"

"No, no," rejoined Juliette hastily; "I'll see to the passports somehow, Pétronelle. Sir Percy Blakeney is English; he'll tell me what to do."

"Do you know where he lives, my jewel?"

"Yes; I heard him tell Madame Déroulède last night that he was lodging with a provincial named Brogard at the Sign of the Cruche Cassée. I'll go seek him, Pétronelle; I am sure he will help me. The English are so resourceful and practical. He'll get us our passports, I know, and advise us as to the best way to proceed. Do you stay here and get all our things ready. I'll not be long."

She took up a cloak and hood, and, throwing them over her arm, she slipped out of the room.

Déroulède had left the house earlier in the day. She hoped that he had not yet returned, and ran down the stairs quickly, so that she might go out unperceived.

The house was quite peaceful and still. It seemed strange to Juliette that there did not hang over it some sort of pall-like presentiment of coming evil.

From the kitchen, at some little distance from the hall, Anne Mie's voice was heard singing an old ditty:

> "De ta tige détachée
> Pauvre feuille désséchée
> Où vas-tu?"

Juliette paused a moment. An awful ache had seized her heart; her eyes unconsciously filled with tears, as they roamed round the walls of this house which had sheltered her so hospitably, these three weeks past.

And now whither was she going? Like the poor, dead leaf of the song, she was wastrel, torn from the parent bough, homeless, friendless, having turned against the one hand which, in this great time of peril, had been extended to her in kindness and in love.

Conscience was beginning to rise up against her, and that hydra-headed tyrant Remorse. She closed her eyes to shut out the hideous vision of her crime; she tried to forget this home which her treachery had desecrated.

> "Je vais où va toute chose
> Où va la feuille de rose
> Et la feuille de laurier,"

sang Anne Mie plaintively.

A great sob broke from Juliette's aching heart. The misery of it all was more than she could bear. Ah, pity her if you can! She had fought and striven, and been conquered. A girl's soul is so young, so impressionable; and she had grown up with that one, awful, all-pervading idea of duty to accomplish, a most solemn oath to fulfil, one sworn to her dying father, and on the dead body of her brother. She had begged for guidance, prayed for release, and the voice from above had remained silent. Weak, miserable, cringing, the human soul, when torn with earthly passion, must look at its own strength for the fight.

And now the end had come. That swift, scarce tangible dream of peace, which had flitted through her mind during the past few weeks, had vanished with the dawn, and she was left desolate, alone with her great sin and its lifelong expiation.

Scarce knowing what she did, she fell on her knees, there on that threshold, which she was about to leave for ever. Fate had placed on her young shoulders a burden too heavy for her to bear.

"Juliette!"

At first she did not move. It was his voice coming from the study behind her. Its magic thrilled her, as it had done that day in the Hall of Justice. Strong, passionate, tender, it seemed now to raise every echo of response in her heart. She thought it was a dream, and remained there on her knees lest it should be dispelled.

Then she heard his footsteps on the flagstones of the hall. Anne Mie's plaintive singing had died away in the distance. She started, and jumped to her feet, hastily drying her eyes. The momentary dream was dispelled, and she was ashamed of her weakness.

He, the cause of all her sorrows, of her sin, and of her degradation, had no right to see her suffer.

She would have fled out of the house now, but it was too late. He had come out of his study, and, seeing her there on her knees weeping, he came quickly forward, trying, with all the innate chivalry of his upright nature, not to let her see that he had been a witness to her tears.

"You are going out, mademoiselle?" he said courteously, as, wrapping her cloak around her, she was turning towards the door.

"Yes, yes," she replied hastily; "a small errand, I ..."

"Is it anything I can do for you?"

"No."

"If ..." he added, with visible embarrassment, "if your errand would brook a delay, might I crave the honour of your presence in my study for a few moments?"

"My errand brooks of no delay, Citizen Déroulède," she said as composedly as she could, "and perhaps on my return I might ..."

"I am leaving almost directly, mademoiselle, and I would wish to bid you good-bye."

He stood aside to allow her to pass, either out, through the street door or across the hall to his study.

There had been no reproach in his voice towards the guest, who was thus leaving him without a word of farewell. Perhaps if there had been any, Juliette would have rebelled. As it was, an unconquerable magnetism seemed to draw her towards him, and, making an almost imperceptible sign of acquiescence, she glided past him into his room.

The study was dark and cool; for the room faced the west, and the shutters had been closed, in order to keep out the hot August sun. At first Juliette could see nothing, but she felt his presence near her, as he followed her into the room, leaving the door slightly ajar.

"It is kind of you, mademoiselle," he said gently, "to accede to my request, which was perhaps presumptuous. But, you see, I am leaving this house to-day, and I had a selfish longing to hear your voice bidding me farewell."

Juliette's large, burning eyes were gradually piercing the semi-gloom around her. She could see him distinctly now, standing

49

close beside her, in an attitude of the deepest, almost reverential respect.

The study was as usual neat and tidy, denoting the orderly habits of a man of action and energy. On the ground there was a valise, ready strapped as if for a journey, and on the top of it a bulky letter-case of stout pigskin, secured with a small steel lock. Juliette's eyes fastened upon this case with a look of fascination and of horror. Obviously it contained Déroulède's papers, the plans for Marie Antoinette's escape, the passports of which he had spoken the day before to his friend, Sir Percy Blakeney—the proofs, in fact, which she had offered to the representatives of the people, in support of her denunciation of the Citizen-Deputy.

After his request he had said nothing more. He was waiting for her to speak; but her voice felt parched; it seemed to her as if hands of steel were gripping her throat, smothering the words she would have longed to speak.

"Will you not wish me godspeed, mademoiselle?" he repeated gently.

"Godspeed?" Oh! the awful irony of it all! Should God speed him to a mock trial and to the guillotine? He was going thither, though he did not know it, and was even now trying to take the hand which had deliberately sent him there.

At last she made an effort to speak, and in a toneless, even voice she contrived to murmur:

"You are not going for long, Citizen-Deputy?"

"In these times, mademoiselle," he replied, "any farewell might be for ever. But I am actually going for a month to the Conciergerie, to take charge of the unfortunate prisoner there."

"For a month!" she repeated mechanically.

"Oh yes!" he said, with a smile. "You see, our present Government is afraid that poor Marie Antoinette will exercise her fascinations over any lieutenant-governor of her prison, if he remain near her long enough, so a new one is appointed every month. I shall be in charge during this coming Vendémiaire. I shall hope to return before the equinox, but—who can tell?"

"In any case then, Citoyen Déroulède, the farewell I bid you to-night will be a very long one."

"A month will seem a century to me," he said earnestly, "since I must spend it without seeing you, but ..."

He looked long and searchingly at her. He did not understand her in her present mood, so scared and wild did she seem, so unlike that girlish, light-hearted self, which had made the dull old house so bright these past few weeks.

50

"But I should not dare to hope," he murmured, "that a similar reason would cause you to call that month a long one."

She turned perhaps a trifle paler than she had been hitherto, and her eyes roamed round the room like those of a trapped hare seeking to escape.

"You misunderstand me, Citoyen Déroulède," she said at last hurriedly. "You have all been kind—very kind—but Pétronelle and I can no longer trespass on your hospitality. We have friends in England, and many enemies here ..."

"I know," he interrupted quietly; "it would be the most arrant selfishness on my part to suggest, that you should stay here an hour longer than necessary. I fear that after to-day my roof may no longer prove a sheltering one for you. But will you allow me to arrange for your safety, as I am arranging for that of my mother and Anne Mie? My English friend Sir Percy Blakeney, has a yacht in readiness off the Normandy coast. I have already seen to your passports and to all the arrangements of your journey as far as there, and Sir Percy, or one of his friends, will see you safely on board the English yacht. He has given me his promise that he will do this, and I trust him as I would myself. For the journey through France, my name is a sufficient guarantee that you will be unmolested; and if you will allow it, my mother and Anne Mie will travel in your company. Then..."

"I pray you stop, Citizen Déroulède," she suddenly interrupted excitedly. "You must forgive me, but I cannot allow thus to make any arrangements for me. Pétronelle and I must do as best we can. All your time and trouble should be spent for the benefit of those who have a claim upon you, whilst I ..."

"You speak unkindly, mademoiselle; there is no question of claim."

"And you have no right to think ..." she continued, with a growing, nervous excitement, drawing her hand hurriedly away, for he had tried to seize it.

"Ah! pardon me," he interrupted earnestly, "there you are wrong. I have the right to think of you and for you—the inalienable right conferred upon me by my great love for you."

"Citizen-Deputy!"

"Nay, Juliette; I know my folly, and I know my presumption. I know the pride of your caste and of your party, and how much you despise the partisan of the squalid mob of France. Have I said that I aspired to gain your love? I wonder if I have ever dreamed it? I only know, Juliette, that you are to me something akin to the angels, something white and ethereal, intangible, and perhaps ununderstandable. Yet, knowing my folly, I glory in it, my dear, and

51

I would not let you go out of my life without telling you of that, which has made every hour of the past few weeks a paradise for me—my love for you, Juliette."

He spoke in that low, impressive voice of his, and with those soft, appealing tones with which she had once heard him pleading for poor Charlotte Corday. Yet now he was not pleading for himself, not for his selfish wish or for his own happiness, only pleading for his love, that she should know of it, and, knowing it, have pity in her heart for him, and let him serve her to the end.

He did not say anything more for a while; he had taken her hand, which she no longer withdrew from him, for there was sweet pleasure in feeling his strong fingers close tremblingly over hers. He pressed his lips upon her hand, upon the soft palm and delicate wrist, his burning kisses bearing witness to the tumultuous passion, which his reverence for her was holding in check.

She tried to tear herself away from him, but he would not let her go:

"Do not go away just yet, Juliette," he pleaded. "Think! I may never see you again; but when you are far from me—in England, perhaps— amongst your own kith and kin, will you try sometimes to think kindly of one who so wildly, so madly worships you?"

She would have stilled, an she could, the beating of her heart, which went out to him at last with all the passionate intensity of her great, pent-up love. Every word he spoke had its echo within her very soul, and she tried not to hear his tender appeal, not to see his dark head bending in worship before her. She tried to forget his presence, not to know that he was there—he, the man whom she had betrayed to serve her own miserable vengeance, whom in her mad, exalted rage she had thought that she hated, but whom she now knew that she loved better than her life, better than her soul, her traditions, or her oath.

Now, at this moment, she made every effort to conjure up the vision of her brother brought home dead upon a stretcher, of her father's declining years, rendered hideous by the mind unhinged through the great sorrow.

She tried to think of the avenging finger of God pointing the way to the fulfilment of her oath, and called to Him to stand by her in this terrible agony of her soul.

And God spoke to her at last; through the eternal vistas of boundless universe, from that heaven which had known no pity, His voice came to her now, clear, awesome, and implacable:

"Vengeance is mine! I will repay!"

52

CHAPTER XII

THE SWORD OF DAMOCLES

"In the name of the Republic!"

Absorbed in his thoughts, his dreams, his present happiness, Déroulède had heard nothing of what was going on in the house, during the past few seconds.

At first, to Anne Mie, who was still singing her melancholy ditty over her work in the kitchen, there had seemed nothing unusual in the peremptory ring at the front-door bell. She pulled down her sleeves over her thin arms, smoothed down her cooking apron, then only did she run to see who the visitor might be.

As soon as she had opened the door, however, she understood.

Five men were standing before her, four of whom wore the uniform of the National Guard, and the fifth, the tricolour scarf fringed with gold, which denoted service under the Convention.

This man seemed to be in command of the others, and he immediately stepped into the hall, followed by his four companions, who at a sign from him, effectively cut off Anne Mie from what had been her imminent purpose—namely, to run to the study and warn Déroulède of his danger.

That it was danger of the most certain, the most deadly kind she never doubted for one moment. Even had her instinct not warned her, she would have guessed. One glance at the five men had sufficed to tell her: their attitude, their curt word of command, their air of authority as they crossed the hall—everything revealed the purpose of their visit: a domiciliary search in the house of Citizen-Deputy Déroulède.

Merlin's Law of the Suspect was in full operation. Someone had denounced the Citizen-Deputy to the Committee of Public Safety; and in this year of grace, 1793, and I. of the Revolution, men and women were daily sent to the guillotine on suspicion.

Anne Mie would have screamed, had she dared, but instinct such as hers was far too keen, to betray her into so injudicious an act. She felt that, were Paul Déroulède's eyes upon her at this moment, he would wish her to remain calm and outwardly serene.

The foremost man—he with the tricolour scarf—had already crossed the hall, and was standing outside the study door. It was his word of command which first roused Déroulède from his dream:

"In the name of the Republic!"

Déroulède did not immediately drop the small hand, which a moment ago he had been covering with kisses. He held it to his lips once more, very gently, lingering over this last fond caress, as if over an eternal farewell, then he straightened out his broad, well-knit figure, and turned to the door.

He was very pale, but there was neither fear nor even surprise expressed in his earnest, deep-set eyes. They still seemed to be looking afar, gazing upon a heaven-born vision, which the touch of her hand and the avowal of his love had conjured up before him.

"In the name of the Republic!"

Once more, for the third time—according to custom—the words rang out, clear, distinct, peremptory.

In that one fraction of a second, whilst those six words were spoken, Déroulède's eyes wandered swiftly towards the heavy letter-case, which now held his condemnation, and a wild, mad thought—the mere animal desire to escape from danger—surged up in his brain.

The plans for the escape of Marie Antoinette, the various passports, worded in accordance with the possible disguises the unfortunate Queen might assume—all these papers were more than sufficient proof of what would be termed his treason against the Republic.

He could already hear the indictment against him, could see the filthy mob of Paris dancing a wild saraband round the tumbril, which bore him towards the guillotine; he could hear their yells of execration, could feel the insults hurled against him, by those who had most admired, most envied him. And from all this he would have escaped if he could, if it had not been too late.

It was but a second, or less, whilst the words were spoken outside his door, and whilst all other thoughts in him were absorbed in this one mad desire for escape. He even made a movement, as if to snatch up the letter-case and to hide it about his person. But it was heavy and bulky; it would be sure to attract attention, and might bring upon him the additional indignity of being forced to submit to a personal search.

He caught Juliette's eyes fixed upon him with an intensity of gaze which, in that same one mad moment, revealed to him the depths of her love. Then the second's weakness was gone; he was once more quiet, firm, the man of action, accustomed to meet danger boldly, to rule and to subdue the most turgid mob.

With a quiet shrug of the shoulders, he dismissed all thought of the compromising lettercase, and went to the door.

Already, as no reply had come to the third word of command,

it had been thrown open from outside, and Déroulède found himself face to face with the five men.

"Citizen Merlin!" he said quietly, as he recognised the foremost among them.

"Himself, Citizen-Deputy," rejoined the latter, with a sneer, "at your service."

Anne Mie, in a remote corner of the hall, had heard the name, and felt her very soul sicken at its sound.

Merlin! Author of that infamous Law of the Suspect which had set man against man, a father against his son, brother against brother, and friend against friend, had made of every human creature a bloodhound on the track of his fellowmen, dogging in order not to be dogged, denouncing, spying, hounding, in order not to be denounced.

And he, Merlin, gloried in this, the most fiendishly evil law ever perpetrated for the degradation of the human race.

There is that sketch of him in the Musée Carnavalet, drawn just before he, in his turn, went to expiate his crimes on that very guillotine, which he had sharpened and wielded so powerfully against his fellows. The artist has well caught the slouchy, slovenly look of his loosely knit figure, his long limbs and narrow head, with the snakelike eyes and slightly receding chin. Like Marat, his model and prototype, Merlin affected dirty, ragged clothes. The real Sanscullottism, the downward levelling of his fellowmen to the lowest rung of the social ladder, pervaded every action of this noted product of the great Revolution.

Even Déroulède, whose entire soul was filled with a great, all-understanding pity for the weaknesses of mankind, recoiled at sight of this incarnation of the spirit of squalor and degradation, of all that was left of the noble Utopian theories of the makers of the Revolution.

Merlin grinned when he saw Déroulède standing there, calm, impassive, well dressed, as if prepared to receive an honoured guest, rather than a summons to submit to the greatest indignity a proud man has ever been called upon to suffer.

Merlin had always hated the popular Citizen-Deputy. Friend and boon-companion of Marat and his gang, he had for over two years now exerted all the influence he possessed in order to bring Déroulède under a cloud of suspicion.

But Déroulède had the ear of the populace. No one understood as he did the tone of a Paris mob; and the National Convention, ever terrified of the volcano it had kindled, felt that a popular member of its assembly was more useful alive than dead.

But now at last Merlin was having his way. An anonymous

denunciation against Déroulède had reached the Public Prosecutor that day. Tinville and Merlin were the fastest of friends, so the latter easily obtained the privilege of being the first to proclaim to his hated enemy, the news of his downfall.

He stood facing Déroulède for a moment, enjoying the present situation to its full. The light from the vast hall struck full upon the powerful figure of the Citizen-Deputy and upon his firm, dark face and magnetic, restless eyes. Behind him the study, with its closely-drawn shutters, appeared wrapped in gloom.

Merlin turned to his men, and, still delighted with his position of a cat playing with a mouse, he pointed to Déroulède, with a smile and a shrug of the shoulders.

"Voyez-moi donc çà, " he said, with a coarse jest, and expectorating contemptuously upon the floor, "the aristocrat seems not to understand that we are here in the name of the Republic. There is a very good proverb, Citizen-Deputy," he added, once more addressing Déroulède, "which you seem to have forgotten, and that is that the pitcher which goes too often to the well breaks at last. You have conspired against the liberties of the people for the past ten years. Retribution has come to you at last; the people of France have come to their senses. The National Convention wants to know what treason you are hatching between these four walls, and it has deputed me to find out all there is to know."

"At your service, Citizen-Deputy!" said Déroulède, quietly stepping aside, in order to make way for Merlin and his men.

Resistance was useless, and, like all strong, determined natures, he knew when it was best to give in.

During this while, Juliette had neither moved nor uttered a sound. Little more than a minute had elapsed since the moment when the first peremptory order, to open in the name of the Republic, had sounded like the tocsin through the stillness of the house. Déroulède's kisses were still hot upon her hand, his words of love were still ringing in her ears.

And now this awful, deadly peril, which she with her own hand had brought on the man she loved!

If in one moment's anguish the soul be allowed to expiate a lifelong sin, then indeed did Juliette atone during this one terrible second.

Her conscience, her heart, her entire being rose in revolt against her crime. Her oath, her life, her final denunciation appeared before her in all their hideousness.

And now it was too late.

Déroulède stood facing Merlin, his most implacable enemy. The latter was giving orders to his men, preparatory to searching the house, and there, just on the top of the valise, lay the letter-case, obviously containing those papers, to which the day before she had overheard Déroulède making allusion, whilst he spoke to his friend, Sir Percy Blakeney.

An unexplainable instinct seemed to tell her that the papers were in that case. Her eyes were riveted on it, as if fascinated. An awful terror held her enthralled for one second more, whilst her thoughts, her longings, her desires were all centred on the safety of that one thing.

The next instant she had seized it and thrown it upon the sofa. Then seating herself beside it, with the gesture of a queen and the grace of a Parisienne, she had spread the ample folds of her skirts over the compromising case, hiding it entirely from view.

Merlin in the hall was ordering two men to stand one on each side of Déroulède, and two more to follow him into the room. Now he entered it himself, his narrow eyes trying to pierce the semi-obscurity, which was rendered more palpable by the brilliant light in the hall.

He had not seen Juliette's gesture, but he had heard the frou-frou of her skirts, as she seated herself upon the sofa.

"You are not alone Citizen-Deputy, I see," he said, with a sneer, as his snakelike eyes lighted upon the young girl.

"My guest, Citizen Merlin," replied Déroulède as calmly as he could— "Citizen Juliette Marny. I know that it is useless, under these circumstances, to ask for consideration for a woman, but I pray you to remember, as far as is possible, that although we are all Republicans, we are also Frenchmen, and all still equal in our sentiment of chivalry towards our mothers, our sisters, or our guests."

Merlin chuckled, and gazed for a moment ironically at Juliette. He had held, between his talon-like fingers, that very morning, a thin scrap of paper, on which a schoolgirlish hand had scrawled the denunciation against Citizen-Deputy Déroulède.

Coarse in nature, and still coarser in thoughts, this representative of the people had very quickly arrived at a conclusion in his mind, with regard to this so-called guest in the Déroulède household.

"A discarded mistress," he muttered to himself. "Just had another scene, I suppose. He's got tired of her, and she's given him away out of spite."

Satisfied with this explanation of the situation, he was quite inclined to be amiable to Juliette. Moreover, he had caught sight of the valise, and almost thought that the young girl's eyes had directed his attention towards it.

"Open those shutters!" he commanded, "this place is like a vault."

One of the men obeyed immediately, and as the brilliant August sun came streaming into the room, Merlin once more turned to Déroulède.

"Information has been laid against you, Citizen-Deputy," he said, "by an anonymous writer, who states that you have just now in your possession correspondence or other papers intended for the Widow Capet: and the Committee of Public Safety has entrusted me and these citizens to seize such correspondence, and make you answerable for its presence in your house."

Déroulède hesitated for one brief fraction of a second. As soon as the shutters had been opened, and the room flooded in daylight, he had at once perceived that his letter-case had disappeared, and guessed, from Juliette's attitude upon the sofa, that she had concealed it about her person. It was this which caused him to hesitate.

His heart was filled with boundless gratitude to her for her noble effort to save him, but he would have given his life at this moment, to undo what she had done.

The Terrorists were no respecters of persons or of sex. A domicillary search order, in those days, conferred full powers on those in authority, and Juliette might at any moment now be peremptorily ordered to rise. Through her action she had made herself one with the Citizen-Deputy; if the case were found under the folds of her skirts, she would be accused of connivance, or at any rate of the equally grave charge of shielding a traitor.

The manly pride in him rebelled at the thought of owing his immediate safety to a woman, yet he could not now discard her help, without compromising her irretrievably.

He dared not even to look again towards her, for he felt that at this moment her life as well as his own lay in the quiver of an eyelid; and Merlin's keen, narrow eyes were fixed upon him in eager search for a tremor, a flash, which might betray fear or prove an admission of guilt.

Juliette sat there, calm, impassive, disdainful, and she seemed to Déroulède more angelic, more unattainable even than before. He could have worshipped her for her heroism, her resourcefulness, her quiet aloofness from all these coarse creatures who filled the room with the odour of their dirty clothes, with their rough jests, and their noisome suggestions.

"Well, Citizen-Deputy," sneered Merlin after a while, "you do not reply, I notice."

"The insinuation is unworthy of a reply, citizen," replied

Déroulède quietly; "my services to the Republic are well known. I should have thought that the Committee of Public Safety would disdain an anonymous denunciation against a faithful servant of the people of France."

"The Committee of Public Safety knows its own business best, Citizen-Deputy," rejoined Merlin roughly. "If the accusation prove a calumny, so much the better for you. I presume," he added with a sneer, "that you do not propose to offer any resistance whilst these citizens and I search your house."

Without another word Déroulède handed a bunch of keys to the man by his side. Every kind of opposition, argument even, would be worse than useless.

Merlin had ordered the valise and desk to be searched, and two men were busy turning out the contents of both on to the floor. But the desk now only contained a few private household accounts, and notes for the various speeches which Déroulède had at various times delivered in the assemblies of the National Convention. Among these, a few pencil jottings for his great defence of Charlotte Corday were eagerly seized upon by Merlin, and his grimy, clawlike hands fastened upon this scrap of paper, as upon a welcome prey.

But there was nothing else of any importance. Déroulède was a man of thought and of action, with all the enthusiasm of real conviction, but none of the carelessness of a fanatic. The papers which were contained in the letter-case, and which he was taking with him to the Conciergerie, he considered were necessary to the success of his plans, otherwise he never would have kept them, and they were the only proofs that could be brought up against him.

The valise itself was only packed with the few necessaries for a month's sojourn at the Conciergerie; and the men, under Merlin's guidance, were vainly trying to find something, anything that might be construed into treasonable correspondence with the unfortunate prisoner there.

Merlin, whilst his men were busy with the search, was sprawling in one of the big leather-covered chairs, on the arms of which his dirty finger-nails were beating an impatient devil's tattoo. He was at no pains to conceal the intense disappointment which he would experience, were his errand to prove fruitless.

His narrow eyes every now and then wandered towards Juliette, as if asking for her help and guidance. She, understanding his frame of mind, responded to the look. Shutting her mentality off from the coarse suggestion of his attitude towards her, she played her part with cunning, and without flinching. With a glance here and there, she directed the men in their search. Déroulède himself could scarcely refrain from looking at her; he was puzzled, and vaguely marvelled at the perfection, with which she carried through her rôle to the end.

Merlin found himself baffled.

He knew quite well that Citizen-Deputy Déroulède was not a man to be lightly dealt with. No mere suspicion or anonymous denunciation would be sufficient in his case, to bring him before the tribunal of the Revolution. Unless there were proofs—positive, irrefutable, damnable proofs—of Paul Déroulède's treachery, the Public Prosecutor would never dare to frame an indictment against him. The mob of Paris would rise to defend its idol; the hideous hags, who plied their knitting at the foot of the scaffold, would tear the guillotine down, before they would allow Déroulède to mount it.

This was Déroulède's stronghold: the people of Paris, whom he had loved through all their infamies, and whom he had succoured and helped in their private need; and above all the women of Paris, whose children he had caused to be tended in the hospitals which he had built for them—this they had not yet forgotten, and Merlin knew it. One day they would forget—soon, perhaps—then they would turn on their former idol, and, howling, send him to his death, amidst cries of rancour and execration. When that day came there would be no need to worry about treason or about proofs. When the populace had forgotten all that he had done, then Déroulède would fall.

But that time was not yet.

The men had finished ransacking the room; every scrap of paper, every portable article had been eagerly seized upon.

Merlin, half blind with fury, had jumped to his feet.

"Search him!" he ordered peremptorily.

Déroulède set his teeth, and made no protest, calling up every fibre of moral strength within him, to aid him in submitting to this indignity. At a coarse jest from Merlin, he buried his nails into the palms of his hand, not to strike the foulmouthed creature in the face. But he submitted, and stood impassive by, whilst the pockets of his coat were turned inside out by the rough hands of the soldiers.

All the while Juliette had remained silent, watching Merlin as any hawk would its prey. But the Terrorist, through the very coarseness of his nature, was in this case completely fooled.

He knew that it was Juliette who had denounced Déroulède, and had satisfied himself as to her motive. Because he was low and brutish and degraded, he never once suspected the truth, never saw in that beautiful young woman, anything of the double nature within her, of that curious, self-torturing, at times morbid sense of

60

religion and of duty, at war with her own upright, innately healthy disposition.

The low-born, self-degraded Terrorist had put his own construction on Juliette's action, and with this he was satisfied, since it answered to his own estimate of the human race, the race which he was doing his best to bring down to the level of the beast.

Therefore Merlin did not interfere with Juliette, but contented himself with insinuating, by jest and action, what her share in this day's work had been. To these hints Déroulède, of course, paid no heed. For him Juliette was as far above political intrigue as the angels. He would as soon have suspected one of the saints enshrined in Notre Dame as this beautiful, almost ethereal creature, who had been sent by Heaven to gladden his heart and to elevate his very thought.

But Juliette understood Merlin's attitude, and guessed that her written denunciation had come into his hands. Her every thought, every living sensation within her, was centred in this one thing: to save the man she loved from the consequences of her own crime against him. And for this, even the shadow of suspicion must be removed from him. Merlin's iniquitous law should not touch him again.

When Déroulède at last had been released, after the outrage to which he had been personally subjected, Merlin was literally, and figuratively too, looking about him for an issue to his present dubious position.

Judging others by his own standard of conduct, he feared now that the popular Citizen-Deputy would incite the mob against him, in revenge for the indignities which he had had to suffer. And with it all the Terrorist was convinced that Déroulède was guilty, that proofs of his treason did exist, if only he knew where to lay hands on them.

He turned to Juliette with an unexpressed query in his adder-like eyes. She shrugged her shoulders, and made a gesture as if pointing towards the door.

"There are other rooms in the house besides this," her gesture seemed to say; "try them. The proofs are there, 'tis for you to find them."

Merlin had been standing between her and Déroulède, so that the latter saw neither query nor reply.

"You are cunning, Citizen-Deputy," said Merlin now, turning towards him, "and no doubt you have been at pains to put your treasonable correspondence out of the way. You must understand that the Committee of Public Safety will not be satisfied with a mere

61

examination of your study," he added, assuming an air of ironical benevolence, "and I presume you will have no objection, if I and these citizen soldiers pay a visit to other portions of your house."

"As you please," responded Déroulède drily.

"You will accompany us, Citizen-Deputy," commanded the other curtly.

The four men of the National Guard formed themselves into line outside the study door; with a peremptory nod, Merlin ordered Déroulède to pass between them, then he too prepared to follow. At the door he turned, and once more faced Juliette.

"As for you, citizeness," he said, with a sudden access of viciousness against her, "if you have brought us here on a fool's errand, it will go ill with you, remember. Do not leave the house until our return. I may have some questions to put to you."

CHAPTER XIII

TANGLED MESHES

Juliette waited a moment or two, until the footsteps of the six men died away up the massive oak stairs.

For the first time, since the sword of Damocles had fallen, she was alone with her thoughts.

She had but a few moments at her command in which to devise an issue out of these tangled meshes, which she had woven round the man she loved.

Merlin and his men would return anon. The comedy could not be kept up through another visit from them, and while the compromising letter-case remained in Déroulède's private study he was in imminent danger at the hands of his enemy.

She thought for a moment of concealing the case about her person, but a second's reflection showed her the futility of such a move. She had not seen the papers themselves; any one of them might be an absolute proof of Déroulède's guilt; the correspondence might be in his handwriting.

If Merlin, furious, baffled, vicious, were to order her to be searched! The horror of the indignity made her shudder, but she would have submitted to that, if thereby she could have saved Déroulède. But of this she could not be sure until after she had looked through the papers, and this she had not the time to do.

Her first and greatest idea was to get out of this room, his private study, with the compromising papers. Not a trace of them must be found here, if he were to remain beyond suspicion.

She rose from the sofa, and peeped through the door. The hall was now deserted; from the left wing of the house, on the floor above, the heavy footsteps of the soldiers and Merlin's occasional brutish laugh could be distinctly heard.

Juliette listened for a moment, trying to understand what was happening. Yes; they had all gone to Déroulède's bedroom, which was on the extreme left, at the end of the first-floor landing. There might be just time to accomplish what she had now resolved to do.

As best she could, she hid the bulky leather case in the folds of her skirt. It was literally neck or nothing now. If she were caught on the stairs by one of the men nothing could save her or—possibly—Déroulède.

At any rate, by remaining where she was, by leaving the events

63

to shape themselves, discovery was absolutely certain. She chose to take the risk.

She slipped noiselessly out of the room and up the great oak stairs. Merlin and his men, busy with their search in Déroulède's bedroom, took no heed of what was going on behind them; Juliette arrived on the landing, and turned sharply to her right, running noiselessly along the thick Aubusson carpet, and thence quickly to her own room.

All this had taken less than a minute to accomplish. The very next moment she heard Merlin's voice ordering one of his men to stand at attention on the landing, but by that time she was safe inside her room. She closed the door noiselessly.

Pétronelle, who had been busy all the afternoon packing up her young mistress' things, had fallen asleep in an arm-chair. Unconscious of the terrible events which were rapidly succeeding each other in the house, the worthy old soul was snoring peaceably, with her hands complacently folded on her ample bosom.

Juliette, for the moment, took no notice of her. As quickly and as dexterously as she could, she was tearing open the heavy leather case with a sharp pair of scissors, and very soon its contents were scattered before her on the table.

One glance at them was sufficient to convince her that most of the papers would undoubtedly, if found, send Déroulède to the guillotine. Most of the correspondence was in the Citizen-Deputy's handwriting. She had, of course, no time to examine it more closely, but instinct naturally told her that it was of a highly compromising character.

She gathered the papers up into a heap, tearing some of them up into strips; then she spread them out upon the ash-pan in front of the large earthenware stove, which stood in a corner of the room.

Unfortunately, this was a hot day in August. Her task would have been far easier if she had wished to destroy a bundle of papers in the depth of winter, when there was a good fire burning in the stove.

But her purpose was firm and her incentive, the greatest that has ever spurred mankind to heroism.

Regardless of any consequences to herself, she had but the one object in view, to save Déroulède at all costs.

On the wall facing her bed, and immediately above a velvet-covered prie-dieu, there was a small figure of the Virgin and Child—one of those quaintly pretty devices for holding holy water, which the reverent superstition of the past century rendered a necessary adjunct of every girl's room.

In front of the figure a small lamp was kept perpetually

burning. This Juliette now took between her fingers, carefully, lest the tiny flame should die out. First she poured the oil over the fragments of paper in the ash-pan, then with the wick she set fire to the whole compromising correspondence.

The oil helped the paper to burn quickly; the smell, or perhaps the presence of Juliette in the room caused worthy old Pétronelle to wake.

"It's nothing, Pétronelle," said Juliette quietly; "only a few old letters I am burning. But I want to be alone for a few moments—will you go down to the kitchen until I call you?"

Accustomed to do as her young mistress commanded, Pétronelle rose without a word.

"I have finished putting away your few things, my jewel. There, there! why didn't you tell me to burn your papers for you? You have soiled your dear hands, and ..."

"Sh! Sh! Pétronelle!" said Juliette impatiently, and gently pushing the garrulous old woman towards the door. "Run to the kitchen now quickly, and don't come out of it until I call you. And, Pétronelle," she added, "you will see soldiers about the house perhaps."

"Soldiers! The good God have mercy!"

"Don't be frightened, Pétronelle. But they may ask you questions."

"Questions?"

"Yes; about me."

"My treasure, my jewel," exclaimed Pétronelle in alarm, "have those devils ...?"

"No, no; nothing has happened as yet, but, you know, in these times there is always danger."

"Good God! Holy Mary! Mother of God!"

"Nothing 'll happen if you try to keep quite calm and do exactly as I tell you. Go to the kitchen, and wait there until I call you. If the soldiers come in and question you, if they try to frighten you, remember that we have nothing to fear from men, and that our lives are in God's keeping."

All the while that Juliette spoke, she was watching the heap of paper being gradually reduced to ashes. She tried to fan the flames as best she could, but some of the correspondence was on tough paper, and was slow in being consumed. Pétronelle, tearful but obedient, prepared to leave the room. She was overawed by her mistress' air of aloofness, the pale face rendered ethereally beautiful by the sufferings she had gone through. The eyes glowed large and magnetic, as if in presence of spiritual visions beyond mortal ken;

the golden hair looked like a saintly halo above the white, immaculate young brow.

Pétronelle made the sign of the cross, as if she were in the presence of a saint.

As she opened the door there was a sudden draught, and the last flickering flame died out in the ash-pan. Juliette, seeing that Pétronelle had gone, hastily turned over the few half burnt fragments of paper that were left. In none of them had the writing remained legible. All that was compromising to Déroulède was effectually reduced to dust. The small wick in the lamp at the foot of the Virgin and Child had burned itself out for want of oil; there was no means for Juliette to strike another light and to destroy what remained. The leather case was, of course, still there, with its sides ripped open, an indestructible thing.

There was nothing to be done about that. Juliette after a second's hesitation threw it among her dresses in the valise.

Then she too went out of the room.

CHAPTER XIV

A HAPPY MOMENT

The search in the Citizen-Deputy's bedroom had proved as fruitless as that in his study. Merlin was beginning to have vague doubts as to whether he had been effectively fooled.

His manner towards Déroulède had undergone a change. He had become suave and unctuous, a kind of elephantine irony pervading his laborious attempts at conciliation. He and the Public Prosecutor would be severely blamed for this day's work, if the popular Deputy, relying upon the support of the people of Paris, chose to take his revenge.

In France, in this glorious year of the Revolution, there was but one step between censure and indictment. And Merlin knew it. Therefore, although he had not given up all hope of finding proofs of Déroulède's treason, although by the latter's attitude he remained quite convinced that such proof did exist, he was already reckoning upon the cat's paw, the sop he would offer to that Cerberus, the Committee of Public Safety, in exchange for his own exculpation in the matter.

This sop would be Juliette, the denunciator instead of Déroulède the denounced.

But he was still seeking for the proofs.

Somewhat changing his tactics, he had allowed Déroulède to join his mother in the living-room, and had betaken himself to the kitchen in search of Anne Mie, whom he had previously caught sight of in the hall. There he also found old Pétronelle, whom he could scare out of her wits to his heart's content, but from whom he was quite unable to extract any useful information. Pétronelle was too stupid to be dangerous, and Anne Mie was too much on the alert.

But, with a vague idea that a cunning man might choose the most unlikely places for the concealment of compromising property, he was ransacking the kitchen from floor to ceiling.

In the living-room Déroulède was doing his best to reassure his mother, who, in her turn, was forcing herself to be brave, and not to show by her tears how deeply she feared for the safety of her son. As soon as Déroulède had been freed from the presence of the soldiers, he had hastened back to his study, only to find that Juliette had gone, and that the letter-case had also disappeared. Not knowing what to think, trembling for the safety of the woman he

67

adored, he was just debating whether he would seek for her in her own room, when she came towards him across the landing.

There seemed a halo around her now. Déroulède felt that she had never been so beautiful and to him so unattainable. Something told him then, that at this moment she was as far away from him, as if she were an inhabitant of another, more ethereal planet.

When she saw him coming towards her, she put a finger to her lips, and whispered:

"Sh! sh! the papers are destroyed, burned."

"And I owe my safety to you!"

He had said it with his whole soul, an infinity of gratitude filled his heart, a joy and pride in that she had cared for his safety.

But at his words she had grown paler than she was before. Her eyes, large, dilated, and dark, were fixed upon him with an intensity of gaze which almost startled him. He thought that she was about to faint, that the emotions of the past half hour had been too much for her overstrung nerves. He took her hand, and gently dragged her into the living-room.

She sank into a chair, as if utterly weary and exhausted, and he, forgetting his danger, forgetting the world and all else besides, knelt at her feet, and held her hands in his.

She sat bolt upright, her great eyes still fixed upon him. At first it seemed as if he could not be satiated with looking at her; he felt as if he had never, never really seen her. She had been a dream of beauty to him ever since that awful afternoon when he had held her, half fainting, in his arms, and had dragged her under the shelter of his roof.

From that hour he had worshipped her: she had cast over him the magic spell of her refinement, her beauty, that aroma of youth and innocence which makes such a strong appeal to the man of sentiment.

He had worshipped her and not tried to understand. He would have deemed it almost sacrilege to pry into the mysteries of her inner self, of that second nature in her which at times made her silent, and almost morose, and cast a lurid gloom over her young beauty.

And though his love for her had grown in intensity, it had remained as heaven born as he deemed her to be—the love of a mortal for a saint, the ecstatic adoration of a St Francis for his Madonna.

Sir Percy Blakeney had called Déroulède an idealist. He was that, in the strictest sense, and Juliette had embodied all that was best in his idealism.

It was for the first time to-day, that he had held her hand just

68

for a moment longer than mere conventionality allowed. The first kiss on her finger-tips had sent the blood rushing wildly to his heart; but he still worshipped her, and gazed upon her as upon a divinity.

She sat bolt upright in the chair, abandoning her small, cold hands to his burning grasp.

His very senses ached with the longing to clasp her in his arms, to draw her to him, and to feel her pulses beat closer against his. It was almost torture now to gaze upon her beauty—that small, oval face, almost like a child's, the large eyes which at times had seemed to be blue but which now appeared to be a deep, unfathomable colour, like the tempestuous sea.

"Juliette!" he murmured at last, as his soul went out to her in a passionate appeal for the first kiss.

A shudder seemed to go through her entire frame, her very lips turned white and cold, and he, not understanding, timorous, chivalrous and humble, thought that she was repelled by his ardour and frightened by a passion to which she was too pure to respond.

Nothing but that one word had been spoken—just her name, an appeal from a strong man, overmastered at last by his boundless love—and she, poor, stricken soul, who had so much loved, so deeply wronged him, shuddered at the thought of what she might have done, had Fate not helped her to save him.

Half ashamed of his passion, he bowed his dark head over her hands, and, once more forcing himself to be calm now, he kissed her finger-tips reverently.

When he looked up again the hard lines in her face had softened, and two tears were slowly trickling down her pale cheeks.

"Will you forgive me, madonna?" he said gently. "I am only a man and you are very beautiful. No—don't take your little hands away. I am quite calm now, and know how one should speak to angels."

Reason, justice, rectitude—everything was urging Juliette to close her ears to the words of love, spoken by the man whom she had betrayed. But who shall blame her for listening to the sweetest sound the ears of a woman can ever hear—the sound of the voice of the loved one in his first declaration of love?

She sat and listened, whilst he whispered to her those soft, endearing words, of which a strong man alone possesses the enchanting secret.

She sat and listened, whilst all around her was still. Madame Déroulède, at the farther end of the room, was softly muttering a few prayers.

They were all alone these two in the mad and beautiful world, which man has created for himself—the world of romance—that world more wonderful than any heaven, where only those may enter who have learned the sweet lesson of love. Déroulède roamed in it at will. He had created his own romance, wherein he was as a humble worshipper, spending his life in the service of his madonna.

And she too forgot the earth, forgot the reality, her oath, her crime and its punishment, and began to think that it was good to live, good to love, and good to have at her feet the one man in all the world whom she could fondly worship.

Who shall tell what he whispered? Enough that she listened and that she smiled; and he, seeing her smile, felt happy.

CHAPTER XV

DETECTED

The opening and shutting of the door roused them both from their dreams.

Anne Mie, pale, trembling, with eyes looking wild and terrified, had glided into the room.

Déroulède had sprung to his feet. In a moment he had thrust his own happiness into the background at sight of the poor child's obvious suffering. He went quickly towards her, and would have spoken to her, but she ran past him up to Madame Déroulède, as if she were beside herself with some unexplainable terror.

"Anne Mie," he said firmly, "what is it? Have those devils dared ..."

In a moment reality had come rushing back upon him with full force, and bitter reproaches surged up in his heart against himself, for having in this moment of selfish joy forgotten those who looked up to him for help and protection.

He knew the temper of the brutes who had been set upon his track, knew that low-minded Merlin and his noisome ways, and blamed himself severely for having left Anne Mie and Pétronelle alone with him even for a few moments.

But Anne Mie quickly reassured him.

"They have not molested us much," she said, speaking with a visible effort and enforced calmness. "Pétronelle and I were together, and they made us open all the cupboards and uncover all the dishes. They then asked us many questions."

"Questions? Of what kind?" asked Déroulède.

"About you, Paul," replied Anne Mie, "and about maman, and also about —about the citizeness, your guest."

Déroulède looked at her closely, vaguely wondering at the strange attitude of the child. She was evidently labouring under some strong excitement, and in her thin, brown little hand she was clutching a piece of paper.

"Anne Mie! Child," he said very gently, "you seem quite upset—as if something terrible had happened. What is that paper you are holding, my dear?"

Anne Mie gazed down upon it. She was obviously making frantic efforts to maintain her self-possession.

Juliette at first sight of Anne Mie seemed literally to have been turned to stone. She sat upright, rigid as a statue, her eyes fixed upon the poor, crippled girl as if upon an inexorable judge, about to pronounce sentence upon her of life or death.

Instinct, that keen sense of coming danger which Nature sometimes gives to her elect, had told her that, within the next few seconds, her doom would be sealed; that Fate would descend upon her, holding the sword of Nemesis; and it was Anne Mie's tiny, half-shrivelled hand which had placed that sword into the grasp of Fate.

"What is that paper? Will you let me see it, Anne Mie?" repeated Déroulède.

"Citizen Merlin gave it to me just now," began Anne Mie more quietly; "he seems very wroth at finding nothing compromising against you, Paul. They were a long time in the kitchen, and now they have gone to search my room and Pétronelle's; but Merlin—oh! that awful man!—he seemed like a beast infuriated with his disappointment."

"Yes, yes."

"I don't know what he hoped to get out of me, for I told him that you never spoke to your mother or to me about your political business, and that I was not in the habit of listening at the keyholes."

"Yes. And ..."

"Then he began to speak of—of our guest—but, of course, there again I could tell him nothing. He seemed to be puzzled as to who had denounced you. He spoke about an anonymous denunciation, which reached the Public Prosecutor early this morning. It was written on a scrap of paper, and thrown into the public box, it seems, and ..."

"It is indeed very strange," said Déroulède, musing over this extraordinary occurrence, and still more over Anne Mie's strange excitement in the telling of it. "I never knew I had a hidden enemy. I wonder if I shall ever find out ..."

"That is just what I said to Citizen Merlin," rejoined Anne Mie.

"What?"

"That I wondered if you, or—or any of us who love you, will ever find out who your hidden enemy might be."

"It was a mistake to talk so fully with such a brute, little one."

"I didn't say much, and I thought it wisest to humour him, as he seemed to wish to talk on that subject."

"Well? And what did he say?"

"He laughed, and asked me if I would very much like to know."

"I hope you said No, Anne Mie?"

"Indeed, indeed, I said Yes," she retorted with sudden energy, her eyes fixed now upon Juliette, who still sat rigid and silent, watching every movement of Anne Mie from the moment in which she began to tell her story.

"Would I not wish to know who is your enemy, Paul—the creature who was base and treacherous enough to attempt to deliver you into the hands of those merciless villains? What wrong had you done to anyone?"

"Sh! Hush, Anne Mie! you are too excited," he said, smiling now, in spite of himself, at the young girl's vehemence over what he thought was but a trifle—the discovery of his own enemy.

"I am sorry, Paul. How can I help being excited," rejoined Anne Mie with quaint, pathetic gentleness, "when I speak of such base treachery, as that which Merlin has suggested?"

"Well? And what did he suggest?"

"He did more than suggest," whispered Anne Mie almost inaudibly; "he gave me this paper—the anonymous denunciation which reached the Public Prosecutor this morning—he thought one of us might recognise the handwriting."

Then she paused, some five steps away from Déroulède, holding out towards him the crumpled paper, which up to now she had clutched determinedly in her hand. Déroulède was about to take it from her, and just before he had turned to do so, his eyes lighted on Juliette.

She said nothing, she had merely risen instinctively, and had reached Anne Mie's side in less than the fraction of a second.

It was all a flash, and there was dead silence in the room, but in that one-hundredth part of a second, Déroulède had read guilt in the face of Juliette.

It was nothing but instinct, a sudden, awful, unexplainable revelation. Her soul seemed suddenly to stand before him in all its misery and in all its sin.

It was as if the fire from heaven had descended in one terrific crash, burying beneath its devastating flames his ideals, his happiness, and his divinity. She was no longer there. His madonna had ceased to be.

There stood before him a beautiful woman, on whom he had lavished all the pent-up treasures of his love, whom he had succoured, sheltered, and protected, and who had repaid him thus.

She had forced an entry into his house; she had spied upon him, dogged him, lied to him. The moment was too sudden, too awful for him to make even a wild guess at her motives. His entire life, his whole past, the present, and the future, were all blotted out in this awful dispersal of his most cherished dream. He had forgotten everything else save her appalling treachery; how could he

73

even remember that once, long ago, in fair fight, he had killed her brother?

She did not even try now to hide her guilt.

A look of appeal, touching in its trustfulness, went out to him, begging him to spare her further shame. Perhaps she felt that love, such as his, could not be killed in a flash.

His entire nature was full of pity, and to that pity she made a final appeal, lest she should be humiliated before Madame Déroulède and Anne Mie.

And he, still under the spell of those magic moments when he had knelt at her feet, understood her prayer, and closing his eyes just for one brief moment in order to shut out for ever that radiant vision of a pure angel whom he had worshipped, turned quietly to Anne Mie.

"Give me that paper, Anne Mie," he said coldly. "I may perhaps recognise the handwriting of my most bitter enemy."

"'Tis unnecessary now," replied Anne Mie slowly, still gazing at the face of Juliette, in which she too had read what she wished to read.

The paper dropped out of her hand.

Déroulède stooped to pick it up. He unfolded it, smoothed it out, and then saw that it was blank.

"There is nothing written on this paper," he said mechanically.

"No," rejoined Anne Mie; "no other words save the story of her treachery."

"What you have done is evil and wicked, Anne Mie."

"Perhaps so; but I had guessed the truth, and I wished to know. God showed me this way, how to do it, and how to let you know as well."

"The less you speak of God just now, Anne Mie, the better, I think. Will you attend to maman? she seems faint and ill."

Madame Déroulède, silent and placid in her arm-chair, had watched the tragic scene before her, almost like a disinterested spectator. All her ideas and all her thoughts had been paralysed, since the moment when the first summons at the front door had warned her of the imminence of the peril to her son.

The final discovery of Juliette's treachery had left her impassive. Since her son was in danger, she cared little as to whence that danger had come.

Obedient to Déroulède's wish, Anne Mie was attending to the old lady's comforts. The poor, crippled girl was already feeling the terrible reaction of her deed.

In her childish mind she had planned this way, in which to

74

bring the traitor to shame. Anne Mie knew nothing, cared nothing, about the motives which had actuated Juliette; all she knew was that a terrible Judas-like deed had been perpetrated against the man, on whom she herself had lavished her pathetic, hopeless love.

All the pent-up jealousy which had tortured her for the past three weeks rose up, and goaded her into unmasking her rival.

Never for a moment did she doubt Juliette's guilt. The god of love may be blind, tradition has so decreed it, but the demon of jealousy has a hundred eyes, more keen than those of the lynx.

Anne Mie, pushed aside by Merlin's men when they forced their way into Déroulède's study, had, nevertheless, followed them to the door. When the curtains were drawn aside and the room filled with light, she had seen Juliette enthroned, apparently calm and placid, upon the sofa.

It was instinct, the instinct born of her own rejected passion, which caused her to read in the beautiful girl's face all that lay hidden behind the pale, impassive mask. That same second sight made her understand Merlin's hints and allusions. She caught every inflection of his voice, heard everything, saw everything.

And in the midst of her anxiety and her terrors for the man she loved, there was the wild, primitive, intensely human joy at the thought of bringing that enthroned idol, who had stolen his love, down to earth at last.

Anne Mie was not clever; she was simple and childish, with no complexity of passions or devious ways of intellect. It was her elemental jealousy which suggested the cunning plan for the unmasking of Juliette. She would make the girl cringe and fear, threaten her with discovery, and through her very terror shame her before Paul Déroulède.

And now it was all done; it had all occurred as she had planned it. Paul knew that his love had been wasted upon a liar and a traitor, and Juliette stood pale, humiliated, a veritable wreck of shamed humanity.

Anne Mie had triumphed, and was profoundly, abjectly wretched in her triumph. Great sobs seemed to tear at her very heart-strings. She had pulled down Paul's idol from her pedestal, but the one look she had cast at his face had shown her that she had also wrecked his life.

He seemed almost old now. The earnest, restless gaze had gone from his eyes; he was staring mutely before him, twisting between nerveless fingers that blank scrap of paper, which had been the means of annihilating his dream.

All energy of attitude, all strength of bearing, which were his chief characteristics, seemed to have gone. There was a look of complete blankness, of hopelessness in his listless gesture.

"How he loved her!" sighed Anne Mie, as she tenderly wrapped the shawl round Madame Déroulède's shoulders.

Juliette had said nothing; it seemed as if her very life had gone out of her. She was a mere statue now, her mind numb, her heart dead, her very existence a fragile piece of mechanism. But she was looking at Déroulède. That one sense in her had remained alive: her sight.

She looked and looked: and saw every passing sign of mental agony on his face: the look of recognition of her guilt, the bewilderment at the appalling crash, and now that hideous deathlike emptiness of his soul and mind.

Never once did she detect horror or loathing. He had tried to save her from being further humiliated before his mother, but there was no hatred or contempt in his eyes, when he realised that she had been unmasked by a trick.

She looked and looked, for there was no hope in her, not even despair. There was nothing in her mind, nothing in her soul, but a great pall-like blank.

Then gradually, as the minutes sped on, she saw the strong soul within him make a sudden fight against the darkness of his despair: the movement of the fingers became less listless; the powerful, energetic figure straightened itself out; remembrance of other matters, other interests than his own began to lift the overwhelming burden of his grief.

He remembered the letter-case containing the compromising papers. A vague wonder arose in him as to Juliette's motives in warding off, through her concealment of it, the inevitable moment of its discovery by Merlin.

The thought that her entire being had undergone a change, and that she now wished to save him, never once entered his mind; if it had, he would have dismissed it as the outcome of maudlin sentimentality, the conceit of the fop, who believes his personality to be irresistible.

His own self-torturing humility pointed but to the one conclusion: that she had fooled him all along; fooled him when she sought his protection; fooled him when she taught him to love her; fooled him, above all, at the moment when, subjugated by the intensity of his passion, he had for one brief second ceased to worship in order to love.

When the bitter remembrance of that moment of sweetest folly rushed back to his aching brain, then at last did he look up at her with one final, agonised look of reproach, so great, so tender,

76

and yet so final, that Anne Mie, who saw it, felt as if her own heart would break with the pity of it all.

But Juliette had caught the look too. The tension of her nerves seemed suddenly to relax. Memory rushed back upon her with tumultuous intensity. Very gradually her knees gave beneath her, and at last she knelt down on the floor before him, her golden head bent under the burden of her guilt and her shame.

Déroulède did not attempt to go to her.

Only presently, when the heavy footsteps of Merlin and his men were once more heard upon the landing, she quietly rose to her feet.

She had accomplished her act of humiliation and repentance, there before them all. She looked for the last time upon those whom she had so deeply wronged, and in her heart spoke an eternal farewell to that great, and mighty, and holy love which she had called forth and then had so hopelessly crushed.

Now she was ready for the atonement.

Merlin had already swaggered into the room. The long and arduous search throughout the house had not improved either his temper or his personal appearance. He was more covered with grime than he had been before, and his narrow forehead had almost disappeared beneath the tangled mass of his ill-kempt hair, which he had perpetually tugged forward and roughed up in his angry impatience.

One look at his face had already told Juliette what she wished to know. He had searched her room, and found the fragments of burnt paper, which she had purposely left in the ash-pan.

How he would act now was the one thing of importance left for Juliette to ponder over. That she would not escape arrest and condemnation was at once made clear to her. Merlin's look of sneering contempt, when he glanced towards her, had told her that.

Déroulède himself had been conscious of a feeling of intense relief when the men re-entered the room. The tension had become unendurable. When he saw his dethroned madonna kneel in humiliation at his feet, an overwhelming pain had wrenched his very heart-strings.

And yet he could not go to her. The passionate, human nature within him felt a certain proud exultation at seeing her there.

She was not above him now, she was no longer akin to the angels.

He had given no further thought to his own immediate danger. Vaguely he guessed that Merlin would find the leather case. Where it was he could not tell; perhaps Juliette herself had handed it to the soldiers. She had only hidden it for a few moments, out of impulse perhaps, fearing lest, at the first instant of its discovery, Merlin might betray her.

He remembered now those hints and insinuations which had gone out from the Terrorist to Juliette whilst the search was being conducted in the study. At the time he had merely looked upon these as a base attempt at insult, and had tortured himself almost beyond bearing, in the endeavour to refrain from punishing that evilmouthed creature, who dared to bandy words with his madonna.

But now he understood, and felt his very soul writhing with shame at the remembrance of it all.

Oh yes; the return of Merlin and his men, the presence of these grimy, degraded brutes, was welcome now. He would have wished to crowd in the entire world, the universe and its population, between him and his fallen idol.

Merlin's manner towards him had lost nothing of its ironical benevolence. There was even a touch of obsequiousness apparent in the ugly face, as the representative of the people approached the popular Citizen-Deputy.

"Citizen-Deputy," began Merlin, "I have to bring you the welcome news, that we have found nothing in your house that in any way can cast suspicion upon your loyalty to the Republic. My orders, however, were to bring you before the Committee of Public Safety, whether I had found proofs of your guilt or not. I have found none."

He was watching Déroulède keenly, hoping even at this eleventh hour to detect a look or a sign, which would furnish him with the proofs for which he was seeking. The slightest suggestion of relief on Déroulède's part, a sigh of satisfaction, would have been sufficient at this moment, to convince him and the Committee of Public Safety that the Citizen-Deputy was guilty after all.

But Déroulède never moved. He was sufficiently master of himself not to express either surprise or satisfaction. Yet he felt both— satisfaction not for his own safety, but because of his mother and Anne Mie, whom he would immediately send out of the country, out of all danger; and also because of her, of Juliette Marny, his guest, who, whatever she may have done against him, had still a claim on his protection. His feeling of surprise was less keen, and quite transient. Merlin had not found the letter-case. Juliette, stricken with tardy remorse perhaps, had succeeded in concealing it. The matter had practically ceased to interest him. It was equally galling to owe his betrayal or his ultimate safety to her.

He kissed his mother tenderly, bidding her good-bye, and pressed Anne Mie's timid little hand warmly between his own. He

79

did what he could to reassure them, but, for their own sakes, he dared say nothing before Merlin, as to his plans for their safety.

After that he was ready to follow the soldiers.

As he passed close to Juliette he bowed, and almost inaudibly whispered:

"Adieu!"

She heard the whisper, but did not respond. Her look alone gave him the reply to his eternal farewell.

His footsteps and those of his escort were heard echoing down the staircase, then the hall door to open and shut. Through the open window came the sound of hoarse cheering as the popular Citizen-Deputy appeared in the street.

Merlin, with two men beside him, remained under the portico; he told off the other two to escort Déroulède as far as the Hall of Justice, where sat the members of the Committee of Public Safety. The Terrorist had a vague fear that the Citizen-Deputy would speak to the mob.

An unruly crowd of women had evidently been awaiting his appearance. The news had quickly spread along the streets that Merlin, Merlin himself, the ardent, bloodthirsty Jacobin, had made a descent upon Paul Déroulède's house, escorted by four soldiers. Such an indignity, put upon the man they most trusted in the entire assembly of the Convention, had greatly incensed the crowd. The women jeered at the soldiers as soon as they appeared, and Merlin dared not actually forbid Déroulède to speak.

"A la lanterne, vieux crétin!" shouted one of the women, thrusting her fist under Merlin's nose.

"Give the word, Citizen-Deputy," rejoined another, "and we'll break his ugly face. Nous lui casserons la gueule! "

"A la lanterne! A la lanterne!"

One word from Déroulède now would have caused an open riot, and in those days self defence against the mob was construed into enmity against the people.

Merlin's work, too, was not yet accomplished. He had had no intention of escorting Déroulède himself; he had still important business to transact inside the house which he had just quitted, and had merely wished to get the Citizen-Deputy well out of the way, before he went upstairs again.

Moreover, he had expected something of a riot in the streets. The temper of the people of Paris was at fever heat just now. The hatred of the populace against a certain class, and against certain individuals, was only equalled by their enthusiasm in favour of others.

They had worshipped Marat for his squalor and his vices; they worshipped Danton for his energy and Robespierre for his calm; they worshipped Déroulède for his voice, his gentleness and his pity, for his care of their children and the eloquence of his speech.

It was that eloquence which Merlin feared now; but he little knew the type of man he had to deal with.

Déroulède's influence over the most unruly, the most vicious populace the history of the world has ever known, was not obtained through fanning its passions. That popularity, though brilliant, is always ephemeral. The passions of a mob will invariably turn against those who have helped to rouse them. Marat did not live to see the waning of his star; Danton was dragged to the guillotine by those whom he had taught to look upon that instrument of death as the only possible and unanswerable political argument; Robespierre succumbed to the orgies of bloodshed he himself had brought about. But Déroulède remained master of the people of Paris for as long as he chose to exert that mastery. When they listened to him they felt better, nobler, less hopelessly degraded.

He kept up in their poor, misguided hearts that last flickering sense of manhood which their bloodthirsty tyrants, under the guise of Fraternity and Equality, were doing their best to smother.

Even now, when he might have turned the temper of the small crowd outside his door to his own advantage, he preferred to say nothing; he even pacified them with a gesture.

He well knew that those whom he incited against Merlin now would, once their blood was up, probably turn against him in less than half-an-hour.

Merlin, who all along had meant to return to the house, took his opportunity now. He allowed Déroulède and the two men to go on ahead, and beat a hasty retreat back into the house, followed by the jeers of the women.

"A la lanterne, vieux crétin!" they shouted as soon as the hall door was once more closed in their faces. A few of them began hammering against the door with their fists; then they realised that their special favourite, Citizen-Deputy Déroulède, was marching along between two soldiers, as if he were a prisoner. The word went round that he was under arrest, and was being taken to the Hall of Justice— a prisoner.

This was not to be. The mob of Paris had been taught that it was the master in the city, and it had learned its lesson well. For the moment it had chosen to take Paul Déroulède under its special protection, and as a guard of honour to him—the women in ragged kirtles, the men with bare legs and stripped to the waist, the children all yelling, hooting, and shrieking—followed him, to see that none dared harm him.

81

CHAPTER XVII

ATONEMENT

Merlin waited a while in the hall, until he heard the noise of the shrieking crowd gradually die away in the distance, then with a grunt of satisfaction he one more mounted the stairs.

All these events outside had occurred during a very few minutes, and Madame Déroulède and Anne Mie had been too anxious as to what was happening in the streets, to take any notice of Juliette.

They had not dared to step out on to the balcony to see what was going on, and, therefore, did not understand what the reopening and shutting of the front door had meant.

The next instant, however, Merlin's heavy, slouching footsteps on the stairs had caused Anne Mie to look round in alarm.

"It is only the soldiers come back for me," said Juliette quietly.

"For you?"

"Yes; they are coming to take me away. I suppose they did not wish to do it in the presence of Mr. Déroulède, for fear ..."

She had no time to say more. Anne Mie was still looking at her in awed and mute surprise, when Merlin entered the room.

In his hand he held a leather case, all torn, and split at one end, and a few tiny scraps of half-charred paper. He walked straight up to Juliette, and roughly thrust the case and papers into her face.

"These are yours?" he said roughly.

"Yes."

"I suppose you know where they were found?"

She nodded quietly in reply.

"What were these papers which you burnt?"

"Love letters."

"You lie!"

She shrugged her shoulders.

"As you please," she said curtly.

"What were these papers?" he repeated, with a loud obscene oath which, however, had not the power to disturb the young girl's serenity.

"I have told you," she said: "love letters, which I wished to burn."

"Who was your lover?" he asked.

82

Then as she did not reply he indicated the street, where cries of "Déroulède! Vive Déroulède!" still echoed from afar.

"Were the letters from him?"

"No."

"You had more than one lover, then?"

He laughed, and a hideous leer seemed further to distort his ugly countenance.

He thrust his face quite close to hers, and she closed her eyes, sick with the horror of this contact with the degraded wretch. Even Anne Mie had uttered a cry of sympathy at sight of this evil-smelling, squalid creature torturing, with his close proximity, the beautiful, refined girl before him.

With a rough gesture he put his clawlike hand under her delicate chin, forcing her to turn round and to look at him. She shuddered at the loathsome touch, but her quietude never forsook her for a moment.

It was into the power of wretches such as this man, that she had wilfully delivered the man she loved. This brutish creature's familiarity put the finishing touch to her own degradation, but it gave her the courage to carry through her purpose to the end.

"You had more than one lover, then?" said Merlin, with a laugh which would have pleased the devil himself. "And you wished to send one of them to the guillotine in order to make way for the other? Was that it?"

"Was that it?" he repeated, suddenly seizing one of her wrists, and giving it a savage twist, so that she almost screamed with the pain.

"Yes," she replied firmly.

"Do you know that you brought me here on a fool's errand?" he asked viciously; "that the Citizen-Deputy Déroulède cannot be sent to the guillotine on mere suspicion, eh? Did you know that, when you wrote out that denunciation?"

"No; I did not know."

"You thought we could arrest him on mere suspicion?"

"Yes."

"You knew he was Innocent?"

"I knew it."

"Why did you burn your love letters?"

"I was afraid that they would be found, and would be brought under the notice of the Citizen-Deputy."

"A splendid combination, ma foi! " said Merlin, with an oath, as he turned to the two other women, who sat pale and shrinking in a corner of the room, not understanding what was going on, not knowing what to think or what to believe. They had known nothing of Déroulède's plans for the escape of Marie Antoinette, they didn't know what the letter-case had contained, and yet they both vaguely felt that the beautiful girl, who stood up so calmly before the loathsome Terrorist, was not a wanton, as she tried to make out, but only misguided, mad perhaps—perhaps a martyr.

"Did you know anything of this?" queried Merlin roughly from trembling Anne Mie.

"Nothing," she replied.

"No one knew anything of my private affairs or of my private correspondence," said Juliette coldly; "as you say, it was a splendid combination. I had hoped that it would succeed. But I understand now that Citizen-Deputy Déroulède is a personage of too much importance to be brought to trial on mere suspicion, and my denunciation of him was not based on facts."

"And do you know, my fine aristocrat," sneered Merlin viciously, "that it is not wise either to fool the Committee of Public Safety, or to denounce without cause one of the representatives of the people?"

"I know," she rejoined quietly, "that you, Citizen Merlin, are determined that someone shall pay for this day's blunder. You dare not now attack the Citizen-Deputy, and so you must be content with me."

"Enough of this talk now; I have no time to bandy words with aristos," he said roughly.

"Come now, follow the men quietly. Resistance would only aggravate your case."

"I am quite prepared to follow you. May I speak two words to my friends before I go?"

"No."

"I may never be able to speak to them again."

"I have said No, and I mean No. Now then, forward. March! I have wasted too much time already."

Juliette was too proud to insist any further. She had hoped, by one word, to soften Madame Déroulède's and Anne Mie's heart towards her. She did not know whether they believed that miserable lie which she had been telling to Merlin; she only guessed that for the moment they still thought her the betrayer of Paul Déroulède.

But that one word was not to be spoken. She would have to go forth to her certain trial, to her probable death, under the awful cloud, which she herself had brought over her own life.

She turned quietly, and walked towards the door, where the two men already stood at attention.

Then it was that some heaven-born instinct seemed suddenly to guide Anne Mie. The crippled girl was face to face with a psychological problem, which in itself was far beyond her comprehension, but vaguely she felt that it was a problem. Something in Juliette's face had already caused her to bitterly repent her action towards her, and now, as this beautiful, refined woman was about to pass from under the shelter of this roof, to the cruel publicity and terrible torture of that awful revolutionary tribunal, Anne Mie's whole heart went out to her in boundless sympathy.

Before Merlin or the men could prevent her, she had run up to Juliette, taken her hand, which hung listless and cold, and kissed it tenderly.

Juliette seemed to wake as if from a dream. She looked down at Anne Mie with a glance of hope, almost of joy, and whispered:

"It was an oath—I swore it to my father and my dead brother. Tell him."

Anne Mie could only nod; she could not speak, for her tears were choking her.

"But I'll atone—with my life. Tell him," whispered Juliette.

"Now then," shouted Merlin, "out of the way, hunchback, unless you want to come along too."

"Forgive me," said Anne Mie through her tears.

Then the men pushed her roughly aside. But at the door Juliette turned to her once more, and said:

"Pétronelle—take care of her ..."

And with a firm step she followed the soldiers out of the room.

Presently the front door was heard to open, then to shut with a loud bang, and the house in the Rue Ecole de Médecine was left in silence.

CHAPTER XVIII

IN THE LUXEMBOURG PRISON

Juliette was alone at last—that is to say, comparatively alone, for there were too many aristocrats, too many criminals and traitors, in the prisons of Paris now, to allow of any seclusion of those who were about to be tried, condemned, and guillotined.

The young girl had been marched through the crowded streets of Paris, followed by a jeering mob, who readily recognised in the gentle, high-bred girl the obvious prey, which the Committee of Public Safety was wont, from time to time to throw to the hungry hydra-headed dog of the Revolution.

Lately the squalid spectators of the noisome spectacle on the Place de la Guillotine had had few of these very welcome sights: an aristocrat —a real, elegant, refined woman, with white hands and proud, pale face—mounting the steps of the same scaffold on which perished the vilest criminals and most degraded brutes.

Madame Guillotine was, above all, catholic in her tastes, her gaunt arms, painted blood red, were open alike to the murderer and the thief, the aristocrats of ancient lineage, and the proletariat from the gutter.

But lately the executions had been almost exclusively of a political character. The Girondins were fighting their last upon the bloody arena of the Revolution. One by one they fell still fighting, still preaching moderation, still foretelling disaster and appealing to that people, whom they had roused from one slavery, in order to throw it headlong under a tyrannical yoke more brutish, more absolute than before.

There were twelve prisons in Paris then, and forty thousand in France, and they were all full. An entire army went round the country recruiting prisoners. There was no room for separate cells, no room for privacy, no cause or desire for the most elementary sense of delicacy.

Women, men, children—all were herded together, for one day, perhaps two, and a night or so, and then death would obliterate the petty annoyances, the womanly blushes caused by this sordid propinquity.

Death levelled all, erased everything.

When Marie Antoinette mounted the guillotine she had

forgotten that for six weeks she practically lived day and night in the immediate companionship of a set of degraded soldiery.

Juliette, as she marched through the streets between two men of the National Guard, and followed by Merlin, was hooted and jeered at, insulted, pelted with mud. One woman tried to push past the soldiers, and to strike her in the face—a woman! not thirty!—and who was dragging a pale, squalid little boy by the hand.

"Crache donc sur l'aristo, voyons! " the woman said to this poor, miserable little scrap of humanity as the soldiers pushed her roughly aside. "Spit on the aristocrat!" And the child tortured its own small, parched mouth so that, in obedience to its mother, it might defile and bespatter a beautiful, innocent girl.

The soldiers laughed, and improved the occasion with another insulting jest. Even Merlin forgot his vexation, delighted at the incident.

But Juliette had seen nothing of it all.

She was walking as in a dream. The mob did not exist for her; she heard neither insult nor vituperation. She did not see the evil, dirty faces pushed now and then quite close to her; she did not feel the rough hands of the soldiers jostling her through the crowd: she had gone back to her own world of romance, where she dwelt alone now with the man she loved. Instead of the squalid houses of Paris, with their eternal device of Fraternity and Equality, there were beautiful trees and shrubs of laurel and of roses around her, making the air fragrant with their soft, intoxicating perfumes; sweet voices from the land of dreams filled the atmosphere with their tender murmur, whilst overhead a cloudless sky illumined this earthly paradise.

She was happy—supremely, completely happy. She had saved him from the consequences of her own iniquitous crime, and she was about to give her life for him, so that his safety might be more completely assured.

Her love for him he would never know; now he knew only her crime, but presently, when she would be convicted and condemned, confronted with a few scraps of burned paper and a torn letter-case, then he would know that she had stood her trial, self-accused, and meant to die for him.

Therefore the past few moments were now wholly hers. She had the rights to dwell on those few happy seconds when she listened to the avowal of his love. It was ethereal, and perhaps not altogether human, but it was hers. She had been his divinity, his madonna; he had loved in her that, which was her truer, her better self.

What was base in her was not truly her. That awful oath,

87

sworn so solemnly, had been her relentless tyrant; and her religion—a religion of superstition and of false ideals—had blinded her, and dragged her into crime.

She had arrogated to herself that which was God's alone—"Vengeance!" which is not for man.

That through it all she should have known love, and learned its tender secrets, was more than she deserved. That she should have felt his burning kisses on her hand was heavenly compensation for all she would have to suffer.

And so she allowed them to drag her through the sansculotte mob of Paris, who would have torn her to pieces then and there, so as not to delay the pleasure of seeing her die.

They took her to the Luxembourg, once the palace of the Medici, the home of proud "Monsieur" in the days of the Great Monarch, now a loathsome, overfilled prison.

It was then six o'clock in the afternoon, drawing towards the close of this memorable day. She was handed over to the governor of the prison, a short, thick-set man in black trousers and black-shag woollen shirt, and wearing a dirty red cap, with tricolour rosette on the side of his unkempt head.

He eyed her up and down as she passed under the narrow doorway, then murmured one swift query to Merlin:

"Dangerous?"

"Yes," replied Merlin laconically.

"You understand," added the governor; "we are so crowded. We ought to know if individual attention is required."

"Certainly," said Merlin, "you will be personally responsible for this prisoner to the Committee of Public Safety."

"Any visitors allowed?"

"Certainly not, without the special permission of the Public Prosecutor."

Juliette heard this brief exchange of words over her future fate.

No visitor would be allowed to see her. Well, perhaps that would be best. She would have been afraid to meet Déroulède again, afraid to read in his eyes that story of his dead love, which alone might have destroyed her present happiness.

And she wished to see no one. She had a memory to dwell on—a short, heavenly memory. It consisted of a few words, a kiss—the last one— on her hand, and that passionate murmur which had escaped from his lips when he knelt at her feet:

"Juliette!"

CHAPTER XIX

COMPLEXITIES

Citizen-Deputy Déroulède had been privately interviewed by the Committee of Public Safety, and temporarily allowed to go free.

The brief proceedings had been quite private, the people of Paris were not to know as yet that their favourite was under a cloud. When he had answered all the questions put to him, and Merlin—just returned from his errand at the Luxembourg Prison—had given his version of the domiciliary visitation in the Citizen-Deputy's house, the latter was briefly told that for the moment the Republic had no grievance against him.

But he knew quite well what that meant. He would be henceforth under suspicion, watched incessantly, as a mouse is by the cat, and pounced upon, the moment time would be considered propitious for his final downfall.

The inevitable waning of his popularity would be noted by keen, jealous eyes; and Déroulède, with his sure knowledge of mankind and of character, knew well enough that his popularity was bound to wane sooner or later, as all such ephemeral things do.

In the meanwhile, during the short respite which his enemies would leave him, his one thought and duty would be to get his mother and Anne Mie safely out of the country.

And also ...

He thought of her, and wondered what had happened. As he walked swiftly across the narrow footbridge, and reached the other side of the river, the events of the past few hours rushed upon his memory with terrible, overwhelming force.

A bitter ache filled his heart at the remembrance of her treachery. The baseness of it all was so appalling. He tried to think if he had ever wronged her; wondered if perhaps she loved someone else, and wished him out of her way.

But, then, he had been so humble, so unassuming in his love. He had arrogated nothing unto himself, asked for nothing, demanded nothing in virtue of his protecting powers over her.

He was torturing himself with this awful wonderment of why she had treated him thus.

Out of revenge for her brother's death—that was the only explanation he could find, the only palliation for her crime.

He knew nothing of her oath to her father, and, of course, had never heard of the sad history of this young, sensitive girl placed in one terrible moment between her dead brother and her demented father. He only thought of common, sordid revenge for a sin he had been practically forced to commit.

And how he had loved her! Yes, loved —for that was in the past now.

She had ceased to be a saint or a madonna; she had fallen from her pedestal so low that he could not find the way to descend and grope after the fragments of his ideal.

At his own door he was met by Anne Mie in tears.

"She has gone," murmured the young girl. "I feel as if I had murdered her."

"Gone? Who? Where?" queried Déroulède rapidly, an icy feeling of terror gripping him by the heart-strings.

"Juliette has gone," replied Anne Mie; "those awful brutes took her away."

"When?"

"Directly after you left. That man Merlin found some ashes and scraps of paper in her room ..."

"Ashes?"

"Yes; and a torn letter-case."

"Great God!"

"She said that they were love letters, which she had been burning for fear you should see them."

"She said so? Anne Mie, Anne Mie, are you quite sure?"

It was all so horrible, and he did not quite understand it all; his brain, which was usually so keen and so active, refused him service at this terrible juncture.

"Yes; I am quite sure," continued Anne Mie, in the midst of her tears. "And oh! that awful Merlin said some dastardly things. But she persisted in her story, that she had—another lover. Oh, Paul, I am sure it is not true. I hated her because—because—you loved her so, and I mistrusted her, but I cannot believe that she was quite as base as that."

"No, no, child," he said in a toneless, miserable voice; "she was not so base as that. Tell me more of what she said."

"She said very little else. But Merlin asked her whether she had denounced you so as to get you out of the way. He hinted that— that ..."

"That I was her lover too?"

"Yes," murmured Anne Mie.

She hardly liked to look at him; the strong face had become hard and set in its misery.

"And she allowed them to say all this?" he asked at last.

"Yes. And she followed them without a murmur, as Merlin said she would have to answer before the Committee of Public Safety, for having fooled the representatives of the people."

"She'll answer for it with her life," murmured Déroulède. "And with mine!" he added half audibly.

Anne Mie did not hear him; her pathetic little soul was filled with a great, an overwhelming pity of Juliette and for Paul.

"Before they took her away," she said, placing her thin, delicate-looking hands on his arm. "I ran to her, and bade her farewell. The soldiers pushed me roughly aside; but I contrived to kiss her—and then she whispered a few words to me."

"Yes? What were they?"

"'It was an oath,' she said. 'I swore it to my father and to my dead brother. Tell him,'" repeated Anne Mie slowly.

An oath!

Now he understood, and oh! how he pitied her. How terribly she must have suffered in her poor, harassed soul when her noble, upright nature fought against this hideous treachery.

That she was true and brave in herself, of that Déroulède had no doubt. And now this awful sin upon her conscience, which must be causing her endless misery.

And, alas! the atonement would never free her from the load of self-condemnation. She had elected to pay with her life for her treason against him and his family. She would be arraigned before a tribunal which would inevitably condemn her. Oh! the pity of it all!

One moment's passionate emotion, a lifelong superstition and mistaken sense of duty, and now this endless misery, this terrible atonement of a wrong that could never be undone.

And she had never loved him!

That was the true, the only sting which he knew now; it rankled more than her sin, more than her falsehood, more than the shattering of his ideal.

With a passionate desire for his safety, she had sacrificed herself in order to atone for the material evil which she had done.

But there was the wreck of his hopes and of his dreams!

Never until now, when he had irretrievably lost her, did Déroulède realise how great had been his hopes; how he had watched day after day for a look in her eyes, a word from her lips, to show him that she too —his unattainable saint—would one day come to earth, and respond to his love.

And now and then, when her beautiful face lighted up at sight of him, when she smiled a greeting to him on his return from his work, when she looked with pride and admiration on him from the

91

public bench in the assemblies of the Convention—then he had begun to hope, to think, to dream.

And it was all a sham! A mask to hide the terrible conflict that was raging within her soul, nothing more.

She did not love him, of that he felt convinced. Man like, he did not understand to the full that great and wonderful enigma, which has puzzled the world since primeval times: a woman's heart.

The eternal contradictions which go to make up the complex nature of an emotional woman were quite incomprehensible to him. Juliette had betrayed him to serve her own sense of what was just and right, her revenge and her oath. Therefore she did not love him.

It was logic, sound common-sense, and, aided by his own diffidence where women were concerned, it seemed to him irrefutable.

To a man like Paul Déroulède, a man of thought, of purpose, and of action, the idea of being false to the thing loved, of hate and love being interchangeable, was absolutely foreign and unbelievable. He had never hated the thing he loved or loved the thing he hated. A man's feelings in these respects are so much less complex, so much less contradictory.

Would a man betray his friend? No—never. He might betray his enemy, the creature he abhorred, whose downfall would cause him joy. But his friend? The very idea was repugnant, impossible to an upright nature.

Juliette's ultimate access of generosity in trying to save him, when she was at last brought face to face with the terrible wrong she had committed, that he put down to one of those noble impulses of which he knew her soul to be fully capable, and even then his own diffidence suggested that she did it more for the sake of his mother or for Anne Mie rather than for him.

Therefore what mattered life to him now? She was lost to him for ever, whether he succeeded in snatching her from the guillotine or not. He had but little hope to save her, but he would not owe his life to her.

Anne Mie, seeing him wrapped in his own thoughts, had quietly withdrawn. Her own good sense told her already that Paul Déroulède's first step would be to try and get his mother out of danger, and out of the country, while there was yet time.

So, without waiting for instructions, she began that same evening to pack up her belongings and those of Madame Déroulède.

There was no longer any hatred in her heart against Juliette. Where Paul Déroulède had failed to understand, there Anne Mie had already made a guess. She firmly believed that nothing now could save Juliette from death, and a great feeling of tenderness had crept into her heart, for the woman whom she had looked upon as an enemy and a rival.

She too had learnt in those brief days the great lesson that revenge belongs to God alone.

CHAPTER XX

THE CHEVAL BORGNE

It was close upon midnight.

The place had become suffocatingly hot; the fumes of rank tobacco, of rancid butter, and of raw spirits hung like a vapour in mid-air.

The principal room in the "Auberge du Cheval Borgne" had been used for the past five years now as the chief meeting-place of the ultra-sansculotte party of the Republic.

The house itself was squalid and dirty, up one of those mean streets which, by their narrow way and shelving buildings, shut out sun, air, and light from their miserable inhabitants.

The Cheval Borgne was one of the most wretched-looking dwellings in this street of evil repute. The plaster was cracked, the walls themselves seemed bulging outward, preparatory to a final collapse. The ceilings were low, and supported by beams black with age and dirt.

At one time it had been celebrated for its vast cellarage, which had contained some rare old wines. And in the days of the Grand Monarch young bucks were wont to quit the gay salons of the ladies, in order to repair to the Cheval Borgne for a night's carouse.

In those days the vast cellarage was witness of many a dark encounter, of many a mysterious death; could the slimy walls have told their own tale, it would have been one which would have put to shame the wildest chronicles of M. Vidoq.

Now it was no longer so.

Things were done in broad daylight on the Place de la Révolution: there was no need for dark, mysterious cellars, in which to accomplish deeds of murder and of revenge.

Rats and vermin of all sorts worked their way now in the underground portion of the building. They ate up each other, and held their orgies in the cellars, whilst men did the same sort of thing in the rooms above.

It was a club of Equality and Fraternity. Any passer-by was at liberty to enter and take part in the debates, his only qualification for this temporary membership being an inordinate love for Madame la Guillotine.

It was from the sordid rooms of the Cheval Borgne that most

of the denunciations had gone forth which led but to the one inevitable ending—death.

They sat in conclave here, some twoscore or so at first, the rabid patriots of this poor, downtrodden France. They talked of Liberty mostly, with many oaths and curses against the tyrants, and then started a tyranny, an autocracy, ten thousand times more awful than any wielded by the dissolute Bourbons.

And this was the temple of Liberty, this dark, damp, evil-smelling brothel, with is narrow, cracked window-panes, which let in but an infinitesimal fraction of air, and that of the foulest, most unwholesome kind.

The floor was of planks roughly put together; now they were worm-eaten, bare, save for a thick carpet of greasy dust, which deadened the sound of booted feet. The place only boasted of a couple of chairs, both of which had to be propped against the wall lest they should break, and bring the sitter down upon the floor; otherwise a number of empty wine barrels did duty for seats, and rough deal boards on broken trestles for tables.

There had once been a paper on the walls, now it hung down in strips, showing the cracked plaster beneath. The whole place had a tone of yellowish-grey grime all over it, save where, in the centre of the room, on a rough double post, shaped like the guillotine, a scarlet cap of Liberty gave a note of lurid colour to the dismal surroundings.

On the walls here and there the eternal device, so sublime in conception, so sordid in execution, recalled the aims of the so-called club: "Liberté, Fraternité, Egalité, sinon la Mort."

Below the device, in one or two corners of the room, the wall was further adorned with rough charcoal sketches, mostly of an obscene character, the work of one of the members of the club, who had chosen this means of degrading his art.

To-night the assembly had been reduced to less than a score.

Even according to the dictates of these apostles of Fraternity: "la guillotine va toujours" —the guillotine goes on always. She had become the most potent factor in the machinery of government, of this great Revolution, and she had been daily, almost hourly fed through the activity of this nameless club, which held its weird and awesome sittings in the dank coffee-room of the Cheval Borgne.

The number of the active members had been reduced. Like the rats in the cellars below, they had done away with one another, swallowed one another up, torn each other to pieces in this wild rage for a Utopian fraternity.

Marat, founder of the organisation, had been murdered by a girl's hand; but Charon, Manuel, Osselin had gone the usual way,

95

denounced by their colleagues, Rabaut, Custine, Bison, who in their turn were sent to the guillotine by those more powerful, perhaps more eloquent, than themselves.

It was merely a case of who could shout the loudest at an assembly of the National Convention.

"La guillotine va toujours!"

After the death of Marat, Merlin became the most prominent member of the club—he and Foucquier-Tinville, his bosom friend, Public Prosecutor, and the most bloodthirsty homicide of this homicidal age.

Bosom friend both, yet they worked against one another, undermining each other's popularity, whispering persistently, one against the other: "He is a traitor!" It had become just a neck-to-neck race between them towards the inevitable goal—the guillotine.

Foucquier-Tinville is in the ascendant for the moment. Merlin had been given a task which he had failed to accomplish. For days now, weeks even, the debates of this noble assembly had been chiefly concerned with the downfall of Citizen-Deputy Déroulède. His popularity, his calm security in the midst of this reign of terror and anarchy, had been a terrible thorn in the flesh of these rabid Jacobins.

And now the climax had been reached. An anonymous denunciation had roused the hopes of these sanguinary patriots. It all sounded perfectly plausible. To try and save that traitor, Marie Antoinette, the widow of Louis Capet, was just the sort of scheme that would originate in the brain of Paul Déroulède.

He had always been at heart an aristocrat, and the feeling of chivalry for a persecuted woman was only the outward signs of his secret adherence to the hated class.

Merlin had been sent to search the Deputy's house for proofs of the latter's guilt.

And Merlin had come back empty-handed.

The arrest of a female aristo—the probable mistress of Déroulède, who obviously had denounced him—was but small compensation for the failure of the more important capture.

As soon as Merlin joined his friends in the low, ill-lit, evil-smelling room he realised at once that there was a feeling of hostility against him.

Tinville, enthroned on one of the few chairs of which the Cheval Borgne could boast, was surrounded by a group of surly adherents.

On the rough trestles a number of glasses, half filled with raw potato-spirit, gave the keynote to the temper of the assembly.

All those present were dressed in the black-shag spencer, the

96

seedy black breeches, and down-at-heel boots, which had become recognised as the distinctive uniform of the sansculotte party. The inevitable Phrygian cap, with its tricolour cockade, appeared on the heads of all those present, in various stages of dirt and decay.

Tinville had chosen to assume a sarcastic tone with regard to his whilom bosom friend, Merlin. Leaning both elbows on the table, he was picking his teeth with a steel fork, and in the intervals of his interesting operation, gave forth his views on the broad principles of patriotism.

Those who sat round him felt that his star was in the ascendant and assumed the position of satellites. Merlin as he entered had grunted a sullen "Good-eve," and sat himself down in a remote corner of the room.

His greeting had been responded to with a few jeers and a good many dark, threatening looks. Tinville himself had bowed to him with mock sarcasm and an unpleasant leer.

One of the patriots, a huge fellow, almost a giant, with heavy, coarse fists and broad shoulders that obviously suggested coal-heaving, had, after a few satirical observations, dragged one of the empty wine barrels to Merlin's table, and sat down opposite him.

"Take care, Citizen Lenoir," said Tinville, with an evil laugh, "Citizen-Deputy Merlin will arrest you instead of Deputy Déroulède, whom he has allowed to slip through his fingers."

"Nay; I've no fear," replied Lenoir, with an oath. "Citizen Merlin is too much of an aristo to hurt anyone; his hands are too clean; he does not care to do the dirty work of the Republic. Isn't that so, Monsieur Merlin?" added the giant, with a mock bow, and emphasising the appellation which had fallen into complete disuse in these days of equality.

"My patriotism is too well known," said Merlin roughly, "to fear any attacks from jealous enemies; and as for my search in the Citizen-Deputy's house this afternoon, I was told to find proofs against him, and I found none."

Lenoir expectorated on the floor, crossed his dark hairy arms over the table, and said quietly:

"Real patriotism, as the true Jacobin understands it, makes the proofs it wants and leaves nothing to chance."

A chorus of hoarse murmurs of "Vive la Liberté!" greeted this harangue of the burly coal-heaver.

Feeling that he had gained the ear and approval of the gallery, Lenoir seemed, as it were, to spread himself out, to arrogate to himself the leadership of this band of malcontents, who, disappointed in their lust of Déroulède's downfall, were ready to exult over that of Merlin.

"You were a fool, Citizen Merlin," said Lenoir with slow significance, "not to see that the woman was playing her own game."

Merlin had become livid under the grime on his face. With this ill-kempt sansculotte giant in front of him, he almost felt as if he were already arraigned before that awful, merciless tribunal, to which he had dragged so many innocent victims.

Already he felt, as he sat ensconced behind a table in the far corner of the room, that he was a prisoner at the bar, answering for his failure with his life.

His own laws, his own theories now stood in bloody array against him. Was it not he who had framed the indictments against General Custine for having failed to subdue the cities of the south? against General Westerman and Brunet and Beauharnais for having failed and failed and failed?

And now it was his turn.

These bloodthirsty jackals had been cheated of their prey; they would tear him to pieces in compensation of their loss.

"How could I tell?" he murmured roughly, "the woman had denounced him."

A chorus of angry derision greeted this feeble attempt at defence.

"By your own law, Citizen-Deputy Merlin," commented Tinville sarcastically, "it is a crime against the Republic to be suspected of treason. It is evident, however, that it is quite one thing to frame a law and quite another to obey it."

"What could I have done?"

"Hark at the innocent!" rejoined Lenoir, with a sneer. "What could he have done? Patriots, friends, brothers, I ask you, what could he have done?"

The giant had pushed the wine cask aside, it rolled away from under him, and in the fulness of his contempt for Merlin and his impotence, he stood up before them all, strong in his indictment against treasonable incapacity.

"I ask you," he repeated, with a loud oath, "what any patriot would do, what you or I would have done, in the house of a man whom we all know is a traitor to the Republic? Brothers, friends, Citizen-Deputy Merlin found a heap of burnt paper in a grate, he found a letter-case which had obviously contained important documents, and he asks us what he could do!"

"Déroulède is too important a man to be tried without proofs. The whole mob of Paris would have turned on us for having arraigned him, for having dared lay hands upon his sacred person."

"Without proofs? Who said there were no proofs?" queried Lenoir.

98

"I found the burnt papers and torn letter-case in the woman's room. She owned that they were love letters, and that she had denounced Déroulède in order to be rid of him."

"Then let me tell you, Citizen-Deputy Merlin, that a true patriot would have found those papers in Déroulède's, and not the woman's room; that in the hands of a faithful servant of the Republic those documents would not all have been destroyed, for he would have 'found' one letter addressed to the Widow Capet, which would have proved conclusively that Citizen-Deputy Déroulède was a traitor. That is what a true patriot would have done—what I would have done. Pardi! since Déroulède is so important a personage, since we must all put on kid gloves when we lay hands upon him, then let us fight him with other weapons. Are we aristocrats that we should hesitate to play the part of jackal to this cunning fox? Citizen-Deputy Merlin, are you the son of some ci-devant duke or prince that you dared not forge a document which would bring a traitor to his doom? Nay; let me tell you, friends, that the Republic has no use for curs, and calls him a traitor who allows one of her enemies to remain inviolate through his cowardice, his terror of that intangible and fleeting shadow—the wrath of a Paris mob."

Thunderous applause greeted this peroration, which had been delivered with an accompaniment of violent gestures and a wealth of obscene epithets, quite beyond the power of the mere chronicler to render. Lenoir had a harsh, strident voice, very high pitched, and he spoke with a broad, provincial accent, somewhat difficult to locate, but quite unlike the hoarse, guttural tones of the low-class Parisian. His enthusiasm made him seem impressive. He looked, in his ragged, dust-stained clothes, the very personification of the squalid herd which had driven culture, art, refinement to the scaffold in order to make way for sordid vice, and satisfied lusts of hate.

CHAPTER XXI

A JACOBIN ORATOR

Tinville alone had remained silent during Lenoir's impassioned speech. It seemed to be his turn now to become surly. He sat picking his teeth, and staring moodily at the enthusiastic orator, who had so obviously diverted popular feeling in his own direction. And Tinville brooked popularity only for himself.

"It is easy to talk now, Citizen—er—Lenoir. Is that your name? Well, you are a comparative stranger here, Citizen Lenoir, and have not yet proved to the Republic that you can do ought else but talk."

"If somebody did not talk, Citizen Tinville—is that your name?" rejoined Lenoir, with a sneer—"if somebody didn't talk, nothing would get done. You all sit here, and condemn the Citizen-Deputy Merlin for being a fool, and I must say I am with you there, but ..."

"Pardi! tell us your 'but' citizen," said Tinville, for the coal-heaver had paused, as if trying to collect his thoughts. He had dragged a wine barrel to collect his thoughts. He had dragged a wine barrel close to the trestle table, and now sat astride upon it, facing Tinville and the group of Jacobins. The flickering tallow candle behind him threw into bold silhouette his square, massive head, crowned with its Phrygian cap, and the great breadth of his shoulders, with the shabby knitted spencer and low, turned-down collar.

He had long, thin hands, which were covered with successive coats of coal dust, and with these he constantly made weird gestures, as if in the act of gripping some live thing by the throat.

"We all know that the Deputy Déroulède is a traitor, eh?" he said, addressing the company in general.

"We do," came with uniform assent from all those present.

"Then let us put it to the vote. The Ayes mean death, the Noes freedom."

"Ay, ay!" came from every hoarse, parched throat; and twelve gaunt hands were lifted up demanding death for Citizen-Deputy Déroulède.

"The Ayes have it," said Lenoir quietly, "Now all we need do is to decide how best to carry out our purpose."

Merlin, very agreeably surprised to see public attention thus diverted from his own misdeeds, had gradually lost his surly attitude. He too dragged one of the wine barrels, which did duty for chairs, close to the trestle table, and thus the members of the nameless Jacobin club made a compact group, picturesque in its weird horror, its uncompromising, flaunting ugliness.

"I suppose," said Tinville, who was loth to give up his position as leader of these extremists—"I suppose, Citizen Lenoir, that you are in position to furnish me with proofs of the Citizen-Deputy's guilt?"

"If I furnish you with such proofs, Citizen Tinville," retorted the other, "will you, as Public Prosecutor, carry the indictment through?"

"It is my duty to publicly accuse those who are traitors to the Republic."

"And you, Citizen Merlin," queried Lenoir, "will you help the Republic to the best of your ability to be rid of a traitor?"

"My services to the cause of our great Revolution are too well known -" began Merlin.

But Lenoir interrupted him with impatience.

"Pardi! but we'll have no rhetoric now, Citizen Merlin. We all know that you have blundered, and that the Republic cares little for those of her sons who have failed, but whilst you are still Minister of Justice the people of France have need of you—for bringing other traitors to the guillotine."

He spoke this last phrase slowly and significantly, lingering on the word "other," as if he wished its whole awesome meaning to penetrate well into Merlin's brain.

"What is your advice then, Citizen Lenoir?"

Apparently, by unanimous consent, the coalheaver, from some obscure province of France, had been tacitly acknowledged the leader of the band. Merlin, still in terror for himself, looked to him for advice; even Tinville was ready to be guided by him. All were at one in their desire to rid themselves of Déroulède, who by his clean living, his aloofness from their own hideous orgies and deadly hates, seemed a living reproach to them all; and they all felt that in Lenoir there must exist some secret dislike of the popular Citizen-Deputy, which would give him a clear insight of how best to bring about his downfall.

"What is your advice?" had been Merlin's query, and everyone there listened eagerly for what was to come.

"We are all agreed," commenced Lenoir quietly, "that just at this moment it would be unwise to arraign the Citizen-Deputy without material proof. The mob of Paris worship him, and would turn against those who had tried to dethrone their idol. Now, Citizen Merlin failed to furnish us with proofs of Déroulède's guilt.

For the moment he is a free man, and I imagine a wise one; within two days he will have quitted this country, well knowing that, if he stayed long enough to see his popularity wane, he would also outstay his welcome on earth altogether."

"Ay! Ay!" said some of the men approvingly, whilst others laughed hoarsely at the weird jest.

"I propose, therefore," continued Lenoir after a slight pause, "that it shall be Citizen-Deputy Déroulède himself who shall furnish to the people of France proofs of his own treason against the Republic."

"But how? But how?" rapid, loud and excited queries greeted this extraordinary suggestion from the provincial giant.

"By the simplest means imaginable," retorted Lenoir with imperturbable calm. "Isn't there a good proverb which our grandmothers used to quote, that if you only give a man a sufficient length of rope, he is sure to hang himself? We'll give our aristocratic Citizen-Deputy plenty of rope, I'll warrant, if only our present Minister of Justice," he added, indicating Merlin, "will help us in the little comedy which I propose that we should play."

"Yes! Yes! Go on!" said Merlin excitedly.

"The woman who denounced Déroulède—that is our trump card," continued Lenoir, now waxing enthusiastic with his own scheme and his own eloquence. "She denounced him. Ergo, he had been her lover, whom she wished to be rid of—why? Not, as Citizen Merlin supposed, because he had discarded her. No, no; she had another lover—she has admitted that. She wished to be rid of Déroulède to make way for the other, because he was too persistent—ergo, because he loved her."

"Well, and what does that prove?" queried Tinville with dry sarcasm.

"It proves that Déroulède, being in love with the woman, would do much to save her from the guillotine."

"Of course."

"Pardi! let him try, say I," rejoined Lenoir placidly. "Give him the rope with which to hang himself."

"What does he mean?" asked one or two of the men, whose dull brains had not quite as yet grasped the full meaning of this monstrous scheme.

"You don't understand what I mean, citizens; you think I am mad, or drunk, or a traitor like Déroulède? Eh bien! give me your attention five minutes longer, and you shall see. Let me suppose that we have reached the moment when the woman—what is her name? Oh! ah! yes! Juliette Marny—stands in the Hall of Justice on her trial before the Committee of Public Safety. Citizen Foucquier-

102

Tinville, one of our greatest patriots, reads the indictment against her: the papers surreptitiously burnt, the torn, mysterious letter-case found in her room. If these are presumed, in the indictment, to be treasonable correspondence with the enemies of the Republic, condemnation follows at once, then the guillotine. There is no defence, no respite. The Minister of Justice, according to Article IX of the Law framed by himself, allows no advocate to those directly accused of treason. But," continued the giant, with slow and calm impressiveness, "in the case of ordinary, civil indictments, offences against public morality or matters pertaining to the penal code, the Minister of Justice allows the accused to be publicly defended. Place Juliette Marny in the dock on a treasonable charge, she will be hustled out of the court in a few minutes, amongst a batch of other traitors, dragged back to her own prison, and executed in the early dawn, before Déroulède has had time to frame a plan for her safety or defence. If, then, he tries to move heaven and earth to rescue the woman he loves, the mob of Paris may,—who knows?—take his part warmly. They are mad where Déroulède is concerned; and we all know that two devoted lovers have ere now found favour with the people of France—a curious remnant of sentimentalism, I suppose—and the popular Citizen-Deputy knows better than anyone else on earth, how to play upon the sentimental feelings of the populace. Now, in the case of a penal offence, mark where the difference would be! The woman Juliette Marny, arraigned for wantonness, for an offence against public morals; the burnt correspondence, admitted to be the letters of a lover—her hatred for Déroulède suggesting the false denunciation. Then the Minister of Justice allows an advocate to defend her. She has none in court; but think you Déroulède would not step forward, and bring all the fervour of his eloquence to bear in favour of his mistress? Can you hear his impassioned speech on her behalf?—I can—the rope, I tell you, citizens, with which he'll hang himself. Will he admit in open court that the burnt correspondence was another lover's letters? No!—a thousand times no!—and, in the face of his emphatic denial of the existence of another lover for Juliette, it will be for our clever Public Prosecutor to bring him down to an admission that the correspondence was his, that it was treasonable, that she burnt them to save him."

He paused, exhausted at last, mopping his forehead, then drinking large gulps of brandy to ease his parched throat.

A veritable chorus of enthusiasm greeted the end of his long peroration. The Machiavelian scheme, almost devilish in its cunning, in its subtle knowledge of human nature and of the heart-strings of a noble organisation like Déroulède's, commended itself to these patriots, who were thirsting for the downfall of a superior enemy.

Even Tinville lost his attitude of dry sarcasm; his thin cheeks were glowing with the lust of the fight.

Already for the past few months, the trials before the Committee of Public Safety had been dull, monotonous, uninteresting. Charlotte Corday had been a happy diversion, but otherwise it had been the case of various deputies, who had held views that had become too moderate, or of the generals who had failed to subdue the towns or provinces of the south.

But now this trial on the morrow—the excitement of it all, the trap laid for Déroulède, the pleasure of seeing him take the first step towards his own downfall. Everyone there was eager and enthusiastic for the fray. Lenoir, having spoken at such length, had now become silent, but everyone else talked, and drank brandy, and hugged his own hate and likely triumph.

For several hours, far into the night, the sitting was continued. Each one of the score of members had some comment to make on Lenoir's speech, some suggestion to offer.

Lenoir himself was the first to break up this weird gathering of human jackals, already exulting over their prey. He bad his companions a quiet good-night, then passed out into the dark street.

After he had gone there were a few seconds of complete silence in the dark and sordid room, where men's ugliest passions were holding absolute sway. The giant's heavy footsteps echoed along the ill-paved street, and gradually died away in the distance.

Then at last Foucquier-Tinville, the Public Prosecutor, spoke:

"And who is that man?" he asked, addressing the assembly of patriots.

Most of them did not know.

"A provincial from the north," said one of the men at last; "he has been here several times before now, and last year he was a fairly constant attendant. I believe he is a butcher by trade, and I fancy he comes from Calais. He was originally brought here by Citizen Brogard, who is good patriot enough."

One by one the members of this bond of Fraternity began to file out of the Cheval Borgne. They nodded curt good-nights to each other, and then went to their respective abodes, which surely could not be dignified with the name of home.

Tinville remained one of the last; he and Merlin seemed suddenly to have buried the hatchet, which a few hours ago had threatened to destroy one or the other of these whilom bosom friends.

Two or three of the most ardent of these ardent extremists had gathered round the Public Prosecutor, and Merlin, the framer of the Law of the Suspect.

"What say you, citizens?" said Tinville at last quietly. "That man Lenoir, meseems, is too eloquent—eh?"

"Dangerous," pronounced Merlin, whilst the others nodded approval.

"But his scheme is good," suggested one of the men.

"And we'll avail ourselves of it," assented Tinville, "but afterwards ..."

He paused, and once more everyone nodded approval.

"Yes; he is dangerous. We'll leave him in peace to-morrow, but afterwards ..."

With a gentle hand Tinville caressed the tall double post, which stood in the centre of the room, and which was shaped like the guillotine. An evil look was on his face: the grin of a death-dealing monster, savage and envious. The others laughed in grim content. Merlin grunted a surly approval. He had no cause to love the provincial coal-heaver who had raised a raucous voice to threaten him.

Then, nodding to one another, the last of the patriots, satisfied with this night's work, passed out into the night.

The watchman was making his rounds, carrying his lantern, and shouting his customary cry:

"Inhabitants of Paris, sleep quietly. Everything is in order, everything is at peace."

CHAPTER XXII

THE CLOSE OF DAY

Déroulède had spent the whole of this same night in a wild, impassioned search for Juliette.

Earlier in the day, soon after Anne Mie's revelations, he had sought out his English friend, Sir Percy Blakeney, and talked over with him the final arrangements for the removal of Madame Déroulède and Anne Mie from Paris.

Though he was a born idealist and a Utopian, Paul Déroulède had never for a moment had any illusions with regard to his own popularity. He knew that at any time, and for any trivial cause, the love which the mob bore him would readily turn to hate. He had seen Mirabeau's popularity wane, La Fayette's, Desmoulin's—was it likely that he alone would survive the inevitable death of so ephemeral a thing?

Therefore, whilst he was in power, whilst he was loved and trusted, he had, figuratively and actually, put his house in order. He had made full preparations for his own inevitable downfall, for that probable flight from Paris of those who were dependent upon him.

He had, as far back as a year ago, provided himself with the necessary passports, and bespoken with his English friend certain measures for the safety of his mother and his crippled little relative. Now it was merely a question of putting these measures into execution.

Within two hours of Juliette Marny's arrest, Madame Déroulède and Anne Mie had quitted the house in the Rue Ecole de Médecine. They had but little luggage with them, and were ostensibly going into the country to visit a sick cousin.

The mother of the popular Citizen-Deputy was free to travel unmolested. The necessary passports which the safety of the Republic demanded were all in perfect order, and Madame Déroulède and Anne Mie passed through the north gate of Paris an hour before sunset, on that 24th day of Fructidor.

Their large travelling chaise took them some distance on the North Road, where they were to meet Lord Hastings and Lord Anthony Dewhurst, two of The Scarlet Pimpernel's most trusted lieutenants, who were to escort them as far as the coast, and thence see them safely aboard the English yacht.

On that score, therefore, Déroulède had no anxiety. His chief duty was to his mother and to Anne Mie, and that was now fully discharged.

Then there was old Pétronelle.

Ever since the arrest of her young mistress the poor old soul had been in a state of mind bordering on frenzy, and no amount of eloquence on Déroulède's part would persuade her to quit Paris without Juliette.

"If my pet lamb is to die," she said amidst heart-broken sobs, "then I have no cause to live. Let those devils take me along too, if they want a useless, old woman like me. But if my darling is allowed to go free, then what would become of her in this awful city without me? She and I have never been separated; she wouldn't know where to turn for a home. And who would cook for her and iron out her kerchiefs, I'd like to know?"

Reason and common sense were, of course, powerless in face of this sublime and heroic childishness. No one had the heart to tell the old woman that the murderous dog of the Revolution seldom loosened its fangs, once they had closed upon a victim.

All Déroulède could do was to convey Pétronelle to the old abode, which Juliette had quitted in order to come to him, and which had never been formally given up. The worthy soul, calmed and refreshed, deluded herself into the idea that she was waiting for the return of her young mistress, and became quite cheerful at sight of the familiar room.

Déroulède had provided her with money and necessaries. He had but few remaining hopes in his heart, but among them was the firmly implanted one that Pétronelle was too insignificant to draw upon herself the terrible attention of the Committee of Public Safety.

By the nightfall he had seen the good woman safely installed. Then only did he feel free.

At last he could devote himself to what seemed to him the one, the only, aim of his life—to find Juliette.

A dozen prisons in this vast Paris!

Over five thousand prisoners on that night, awaiting trial, condemnation and death.

Déroulède at first, strong in his own power, his personality, had thought that the task would be comparatively easy.

At the Palais de Justice they would tell him nothing: the list of new arrests had not yet been handled in by the commandant of Paris, Citizen Santerre, who classified and docketed the miserable herd of aspirants for the next day's guillotine.

The lists, moreover, would not be completed until the next

day, when the trials of the new prisoners would already be imminent.

The work of the Committee of Public Safety was done without much delay.

Then began Déroulède's weary quest through those twelve prisons of Paris. From the Temple to the Conciergerie, from Palais Condé to the Luxembourg, he spent hours in the fruitless search.

Everywhere the same shrug of the shoulders, the same indifferent reply to his eager query:

"Juliette Marny? Inconnue. "

Unknown! She had not yet been docketed, not yet classified; she was still one of that immense flock of cattle, sent in ever-increasing numbers to the slaughter-house.

Presently, to-morrow, after a trial which might last ten minutes, after a hasty condemnation and quick return to prison, she would be listed as one of the traitors, whom this great and beneficent Republic sent daily to the guillotine.

Vainly did Déroulède try to persuade, to entreat, to bribe. The sullen guardians of these twelve charnel-houses knew nothing of individual prisoners.

But the Citizen-Deputy was allowed to look for himself. He was conducted to the great vaulted rooms of the Temple, to the vast ballrooms of the Palais Condé, where herded the condemned and those still awaiting trial; he was allowed to witness there the grim farcical tragedies, with which the captives beguiled the few hours which separated them from death.

Mock trials were acted there; Tinville was mimicked; then the Place de la Révolution; Samson the headsman, with a couple of inverted chairs to represent the guillotine.

Daughters of dukes and princes, descendants of ancient lineage, acted in these weird and ghastly comedies. The ladies, with hair bound high over their heads, would kneel before the inverted chairs, and place the snowwhite necks beneath this imaginary guillotine. Speeches were delivered to a mock populace, whilst a mock Santerre ordered a mock roll of drums to drown the last flow of eloquence of the supposed victim.

Oh! the horror of it all—the pity, pathos, and misery of this ghastly parody, in the very face of the sublimity of death!

Déroulède shuddered when first he beheld the scene, shuddered at the very thought of finding Juliette amongst these careless, laughing, thoughtless mimes.

His own, his beautiful Juliette, with her proud face and majestic, queen-like gestures; it was a relief not to see her there.

"Juliette Marny? Inconnue, " was the final word he heard about her.

No one told him that by Deputy Merlin's strictest orders she had been labelled "dangerous," and placed in a remote wing of the Luxembourg Palace, together with a few, who, like herself, were allowed to see no one, communicate with no one.

Then when the couvre-feu had sounded, when all public places were closed, when the night watchman had begun his rounds, Déroulède knew that his quest for that night must remain fruitless.

But he could not rest. In and out the tortuous streets of Paris he roamed during the better part of that night. He was now only awaiting the dawn to publicly demand the right to stand beside Juliette.

A hopeless misery was in his heart, a longing for a cessation of life; only one thing kept his brain active, his mind clear: the hope of saving Juliette.

The dawn was breaking in the far east when, wandering along the banks of the river, he suddenly felt a touch on his arm.

"Come to my hovel," said a pleasant, lazy voice close to his ear, whilst a kindly hand seemed to drag him away from the contemplation of the dark, silent river. "And a demmed, beastly place it is too, but at least we can talk quietly there."

Déroulède, roused from his meditation, looked up, to see his friend, Sir Percy Blakeney, standing close beside him. Tall, débonnair, well-dressed, he seemed by his very presence to dissipate the morbid atmosphere which was beginning to weigh upon Déroulède's active mind.

Déroulède followed him readily enough through the intricate mazes of old Paris, and down the Rue des Arts, until Sir Percy stopped outside a small hostelry, the door of which stood wide open.

"Mine host has nothing to lose from footpads and thieves," explained the Englishman as he guided his friend through the narrow doorway, then up a flight of rickety stairs, to a small room on the floor above. "He leaves all doors open for anyone to walk in, but, la! the interior of the house looks so uninviting that no one is tempted to enter."

"I wonder you care to stay here," remarked Déroulède, with a momentary smile, as he contrasted in his mind the fastidious appearance of his friend with the dinginess and dirt of these surroundings.

Sir Percy deposited his large person in the capacious depths of a creaky chair, stretched his long limbs out before him, and said quietly:

"I am only staying in this demmed hole until the moment when I can drag you out of this murderous city."

Déroulède shook his head.

"You'd best go back to England, then," he said, "for I'll never leave Paris now."

"Not without Juliette Marny, shall we say?" rejoined Sir Percy placidly.

"And I fear me that she has placed herself beyond our reach," said Déroulède sombrely.

"You know that she is in the Luxembourg Prison?" queried the Englishman suddenly.

"I guessed it, but could find no proof."

"And that she will be tried to-morrow?"

"They never keep a prisoner pining too long," replied Déroulède bitterly. "I guessed that too."

"What do you mean to do?"

"Defend her with the last breath in my body."

"You love her still, then?" asked Blakeney, with a smile.

"Still?" The look, the accent, the agony of a hopeless passion conveyed in that one word, told Sir Percy Blakeney all that he wished to know.

"Yet she betrayed you," he said tentatively.

"And to atone for that sin—an oath, mind you, friend, sworn to her father—she is already to give her life for me."

"And you are prepared to forgive?"

"To understand is to forgive," rejoined Déroulède simply, "and I love her."

"Your madonna!" said Blakeney, with a gently ironical smile.

"No; the woman I love, with all her weaknesses, all her sins; the woman to gain whom I would give my soul, to save whom I will give my life."

"And she?"

"She does not love me—would she have betrayed me else?"

He sat beside the table, and buried his head in his hands. Not even his dearest friend should see how much he had suffered, how deeply his love had been wounded.

Sir Percy said nothing, a curious, pleasant smile lurked round the corners of his mobile mouth. Through his mind there flitted the vision of beautiful Marguerite, who had so much loved yet so deeply wronged him, and, looking at his friend, he thought that Déroulède too would soon learn all the contradictions, which wage a constant war in the innermost recesses of a feminine heart.

He made a movement as if he would say something more,

something of grave import, then seemed to think better of it, and shrugged his broad shoulders, as if to say:

"Let time and chance take their course now."

When Déroulède looked up again Sir Percy was sitting placidly in the arm-chair, with an absolutely blank expression on his face.

"Now that you know how much I love her, my friend," said Déroulède as soon as he had mastered his emotions, "will you look after her when they have condemned me, and save her for my sake?"

A curious, enigmatic smile suddenly illumined Sir Percy's earnest countenance.

"Save her? Do you attribute supernatural powers to me, then, or to The League of The Scarlet Pimpernel?"

"To you, I think," rejoined Déroulède seriously.

Once more it seemed as if Sir Percy were about to reveal something of great importance to his friend, then once more he checked himself. The Scarlet Pimpernel was, above all, far-seeing and practical, a man of action and not of impulse. The glowing eyes of his friend, his nervous, febrile movements, did not suggest that he was in a fit state to be entrusted with plans, the success of which hung on a mere thread.

Therefore Sir Percy only smiled, and said quietly:

"Well, I'll do my best."

CHAPTER XXIII

JUSTICE

The day had been an unusually busy one.

Five and thirty prisoners, arraigned before the bar of the Committee of Public Safety, had been tried in the last eight hours—an average of rather more than four to the hour; twelve minutes and a half in which to send a human creature, full of life and health, to solve the great enigma which lies hidden beyond the waters of the Styx.

And Citizen-Deputy Foucquier-Tinville, the Public Prosecutor, had surpassed himself. He seemed indefatigable.

Each of these five and thirty prisoners had been arraigned for treason against the Republic, for conspiracy with her enemies, and all had to have irrefutable proofs of their guilt brought before the Committee of Public Safety. Sometimes a few letters, written to friends abroad, and seized at the frontier; a word of condemnation of the measures of the extremists; and expression of horror at the massacres on the Place de la Révolution, where the guillotine creaked incessantly—these were irrefutable proofs; or else perhaps a couple of pistols, or an old family sword seized in the house of a peaceful citizen, would be brought against a prisoner, as an irrefutable proof of his warlike dispositions against the Republic.

Oh! it was not difficult!

Out of five and thirty indictments, Foucquier-Tinville had obtained thirty convictions.

No wonder his friends declared that he had surpassed himself. It had indeed been a glorious day, and the glow of satisfaction as much as the heat, caused the Public Prosecutors to mop his high, bony cranium before he had adjourned for the much-needed respite for refreshment.

The day's work was not yet done.

The "politicals" had been disposed of, and there had been such an accumulation of them recently that it was difficult to keep pace with the arrests.

And in the meanwhile the criminal record of the great city had not diminished. Because men butchered one another in the name of Equality, there were none the fewer among the Fraternity of thieves and petty pilferers, of ordinary cut-throats and public wantons.

And these too had to be dealt with by law. The guillotine was impartial, and fell with equal velocity on the neck of the proud duke and the gutter-born fille de joie, on a descendant of the Bourbons and the wastrel born in a brothel.

The ministerial decrees favoured the proletariat. A crime against the Republic was indefensible, but one against the individual was dealt with, with all the paraphernalia of an elaborate administration of justice. There were citizen judges and citizen advocates, and the rabble, who crowded in to listen to the trials, acted as honorary jury.

It was all thoroughly well done. The citizen criminals were given every chance.

The afternoon of this hot August day, one of the last of glorious Fructidor, had begun to wane, and the shades of evening to slowly creep into the long, bare room where this travesty of justice was being administered.

The Citizen-President sat at the extreme end of the room, on a rough wooden bench, with a desk in front of him littered with papers.

Just above him, on the bare, whitewashed wall, the words: "La République: une et indivisible, " and below them the device: "Liberté, Egalité, Fraternité! "

To the right and left of the Citizen-President, four clerks were busy making entries in that ponderous ledger, that amazing record of the foulest crimes the world has ever known, the "Bulletin du Tribunal Révolutionnaire. "

At present no one is speaking, and the grating of the clerks' quill pens against the paper is the only sound which disturbs the silence of the hall.

In front of the President, on a bench lower than his, sits Citizen Foucquier-Tinville, rested and refreshed, ready to take up his occupation, for as many hours as his country demands it of him.

On every desk a tallow candle, smoking and spluttering, throws a weird light, and more weird shadows, on the faces of clerks and President, on blank walls and ominous devices.

In the centre of the room a platform surrounded by an iron railing is ready for the accused. Just in front of it, from the tall, raftered ceiling above, there hangs a small brass lamp, with a green abat-jour.

Each side of the long, whitewashed walls there are three rows of benches, beautiful old carved oak pews, snatched from Notre Dame and from the Churches of St Eustache and St Germain l'Auxerrois. Instead of the pious worshippers of mediaeval times, they now accommodate the lookers-on of the grim spectacle of unfortunates, in their brief halt before the scaffold.

113

The front row of these benches is reserved for those citizen-deputies who desire to be present at the debates of the Tribunal Révolutionnaire. It is their privilege, almost their duty, as representatives of the people, to see that the sittings are properly conducted.

These benches are already well filled. At one end, on the left, Citizen Merlin, Minister of Justice, sits; next to him Citizen-Minister Lebrun; also Citizen Robespierre, still in the height of his ascendancy, and watching the proceedings with those pale, watery eyes of his and that curious, disdainful smile, which have earned for him the nickname of "the sea-green incorruptible."

Other well-known faces are there also, dimly outlined in the fast-gathering gloom. But everyone notes Citizen-Deputy Déroulède, the idol of the people, as he sits on the extreme end of a bench on the right, with arms tightly folded across his chest, the light from the hanging lamp falling straight on his dark head and proud, straight brows, with the large, restless, eager eyes.

Anon the Citizen-President rings a hand-bell, and there is a discordant noise of hoarse laughter and loud curses, some pushing, jolting, and swearing, as the general public is admitted into the hall.

Heaven save us! What a rabble! Has humanity really such a scum?

Women with a single ragged kirtle and shift, through the interstices of which the naked, grime-covered flesh shows shamelessly: with bare legs, and feet thrust into heavy sabots, hair dishevelled, and evil, spirit-sodden faces: women without a semblance of womanhood, with shrivelled, barren breasts, and dry, parched lips, that have never known how to kiss. Women without emotion save that of hate, without desire, save for the satisfaction of hunger and thirst, and lust for revenge against their sisters less wretched, less unsexed than themselves. They crowd in, jostling one another, swarming into the front rows of the benches, where they can get a better view of the miserable victims about to be pilloried before them.

And the men without a semblance of manhood. Bent under the heavy care of their own degradation, dead to pity, to love, to chivalry; dead to all save an inordinate longing for the sight of blood.

And God help them all! for there were the children too. Children— save the mark!—with pallid, precocious little faces, pinched with the ravages of starvation, gazing with dim, filmy eyes on this world of rapacity and hideousness. Children who have seen death!

Oh, the horror of it! Not beautiful, peaceful death, a slumber

114

or a dream, a loved parent or fond sister or brother lying all in white amidst a wealth of flowers, but death in its most awesome aspect, violent, lurid, horrible.

And now they stare around them with eager, greedy eyes, awaiting the amusement of the spectacle; gazing at the President, with his tall Phrygian cap; at the clerks wielding their indefatigable quill pens, writing, writing, writing; at the flickering lights, throwing clouds of sooty smoke, up to the dark ceiling above.

Then suddenly the eyes of one little mite—a poor, tiny midget not yet in her teens—alight on Paul Déroulède's face, on the opposite side of the rooms.

"Tiens! Papa Déroulède!" she says, pointing an attenuated little finger across at him, and turning eagerly to those around her, her eyes dilating in wishful recollection of a happy afternoon spent in Papa Déroulède's house, with fine white bread to eat in plenty, and great jars of foaming milk.

He rouses himself from his apathy, and his great earnest eyes lose their look of agonised misery, as he responds to the greeting of the little one.

For one moment—oh! a mere fraction of a second—the squalid faces, the miserable, starved expressions of the crowd, soften at sight of him. There is a faint murmur among the women, which perhaps God's recording angel registered as a blessing. Who knows?

Foucquier-Tinville suppresses a sneer, and the Citizen-President impatiently rings his hand-bell again.

"Bring forth the accused!" he commands in stentorian tones.

There is a movement of satisfaction among the crowd, and the angel of God is forced to hide his face again.

115

CHAPTER XXIV

THE TRIAL OF JULIETTE

It is all indelibly placed on record in the "Bulletin du Tribunal Révolutionnaire," under date 25th Fructidor, year I. of the Revolution.

Anyone who cares may read, for the Bulletin is in the Archives of the Bibliothèque Nationale of Paris.

One by one the accused had been brought forth, escorted by two men of the National Guard in ragged, stained uniforms of red, white, and blue; they were then conducted to the small raised platform in the centre of the hall, and made to listen to the charge brought against them by Citizen Foucquier-Tinville, the Public Presecutor.

They were petty charges mostly: pilfering, fraud, theft, occasionally arson or manslaughter. One man, however, was arraigned for murder with highway robbery, and a woman for the most ignoble traffic, which evil feminine ingenuity could invent.

These two were condemned to the guillotine, the others sent to the galleys at Brest or Toulon—the forger along with the petty thief, the housebreaker with the absconding clerk.

There was no room in the prison for ordinary offences against the criminal code; they were overfilled already with so-called traitors against the Republic.

Three women were sent to the penitentiary at the Salpêtriere, and were dragged out of the court shrilly protesting their innocence, and followed by obscene jeers from the spectators on the benches.

Then there was a momentary hush.

Juliette Marny had been brought in.

She was quite calm, and exquisitely beautiful, dressed in a plain grey bodice and kirtle, with a black band round her slim waist and a soft white kerchief folded across her bosom. Beneath the tiny, white cap her golden hair appeared in dainty, curly profusion; her child-like, oval face was very white, but otherwise quite serene.

She seemed absolutely unconscious of her surroundings, and walked with a firm step up to the platform, looking neither to the right nor to the left of her.

Therefore she did not see Déroulède. A great, a wonderful radiance seemed to shine in her large eyes—the radiance of self-sacrifice.

She was offering not only her life, but everything a woman of refinement holds most dear, for the safety of the man she loved.

A feeling that was almost physical pain, so intense was it, overcame Déroulède, when at last he heard her name loudly called by the Public Prosecutor.

All day he had waited for this awful moment, forgetting his own misery, his own agonised feeling of an irretrievable loss, in the horrible thought of what she would endure, what she would think, when first she realised the terrible indignity, which was to be put upon her.

Yet for the sake of her, of her chances of safety and of ultimate freedom, it was undoubtedly best that it should be so.

Arraigned for conspiracy against the Republic, she was liable to secret trial, to be brought up, condemned, and executed before he could even hear of her whereabouts, before he could throw himself before her judges and take all guilt upon himself.

Those suspected of treason against the Republic forfeited, according to Merlin's most iniquitous Law, their rights of citizenship, in publicity of trial and in defence.

It all might have been finished before Déroulède knew anything of it.

The other way was, of course, more terrible. Brought forth amongst the scum of criminal Paris, on a charge, the horror of which, he could but dimly hope that she was too innocent to fully understand, he dared not even think of what she would suffer.

But undoubtedly it was better so.

The mud thrown at her robes of purity could never cling to her, and at least her trial would be public; he would be there to take all infamy, all disgrace, all opprobrium on himself.

The strength of his appeal would turn her judges' wrath from her to him; and after these few moments of misery, she would be free to leave Paris, France, to be happy, and to forget him and the memory of him.

An overwhelming, all-compelling love filled his entire soul for the beautiful girl, who had so wronged, yet so nobly tried to save him. A longing for her made his very sinews ache; she was no longer madonna, and her beauty thrilled him, with the passionate, almost sensuous desire to give his life for her.

The indictment against Juliette Marny has become history now.

On that day, the 25th Fructidor, at seven o'clock in the evening, it was read out by the Public Prosecutor, and listened to by the accused —so the Bulletin tells us—with complete calm and apparent indifference. She stood up in that same pillory where once

117

stood poor, guilty Charlotte Corday, where presently would stand proud, guiltless Marie Antoinette.

And Déroulède listened to the scurrilous document, with all the outward calm his strength of will could command. He would have liked to rise from his seat then and there, at once, and in mad, purely animal fury have, with a blow of his fist, quashed the words in Foucquier-Tinville's lying throat.

But for her sake he was bound to listen, and, above all, to act quietly, deliberately, according to form and procedure, so as in no way to imperil her cause.

Therefore he listened whilst the Public Prosecutor spoke.

"Juliette Marny, you are hereby accused of having, by a false and malicious denunciation, slandered the person of a representative of the people; you caused the Revolutionary Tribunal, through this same mischievous act, to bring a charge against this representative of the people, to institute a domiciliary search in his house, and to waste valuable time, which otherwise belonged to the service of the Republic. And this you did, not from a misguided sense of duty towards your country, but in wanton and impure spirit, to be rid of the surveillance of one who had your welfare at heart, and who tried to prevent your leading the immoral life which had become a public scandal, and which has now brought you before this court of justice, to answer to a charge of wantonness, impurity, defamation of character, and corruption of public morals. In proof of which I now place before the court your own admission, that more than one citizen of the Republic has been led by you into immoral relationship with yourself; and further, your own admission, that your accusation against Citizen-Deputy Déroulède was false and mischievous; and further, and finally, your immoral and obscene correspondence with some persons unknown, which you vainly tried to destroy. In consideration of which, and in the name of the people of France, whose spokesman I am, I demand that you be taken hence from this Hall of Justice to the Place de la Révolution, in full view of the citizens of Paris and its environs, and clad in a soiled white garment, emblem of the smirch upon your soul, that there you be publicly whipped by the hands of Citizen Samson, the public executioner; after which, that you be taken to the prison of the Salpêtriere, there to be further detained at the discretion of the Committee of Public Safety. And now, Juliette Marny, you have heard the indictment preferred against you, have you anything to say, why the sentence which I have demanded shall not be passed upon you?"

Jeers, shouts, laughter, and curses greeted this speech of the Public Prosecutor.

118

All that was most vile and most bestial in this miserable, misguided people struggling for Utopia and Liberty, seemed to come to the surface, whilst listening to the reading of this most infamous document.

The delight of seeing this beautiful, ethereal woman, almost unearthly in her proud aloofness, smirched with the vilest mud to which the vituperation of man can contrive to sink, was a veritable treat to the degraded wretches.

The women yelled hoarse approval; the children, not understanding, laughed in mirthless glee; the men, with loud curses, showed their appreciation of Foucquier-Tinville's speech.

As for Déroulède, the mental agony he endured surpassed any torture which the devils, they say, reserve for the damned. His sinews cracked in his frantic efforts to control himself; he dug his finger-nails into his flesh, trying by physical pain to drown the sufferings of his mind.

He thought that his reason was tottering, that he would go mad if he heard another word of this infamy. The hooting and yelling of that filthy mob sounded like the cries of lost souls, shrieking from hell. All his pity for them was gone, his love for humanity, his devotion to the suffering poor.

A great, an immense hatred for this ghastly Revolution and the people it professed to free filled his whole being, together with a mad, hideous desire to see them suffer, starve, die a miserable, loathsome death. The passion of hate, that now overwhelmed his soul, was at least as ugly as theirs. He was, for one brief moment, now at one with them in their inordinate lust for revenge.

Only Juliette throughout all this remained calm, silent, impassive.

She had heard the indictment, heard the loathsome sentence, for her white cheeks had gradually become ashy pale, but never for a moment did she depart from her attitude of proud aloofness.

She never once turned her head towards the mob who insulted her. She waited in complete passiveness until the yelling and shouting had subsided, motionless save for her finger-tips, which beat an impatient tattoo upon the railing in front of her.

The Bulletin says that she took out her handkerchief and wiped her face with it. Elle s'essuya le front qui fut perlé de sueur. The heat had become oppressive.

The atmosphere was overcharged with the dank, penetrating odour of steaming, dirty clothes. The room, though vast, was close and suffocating, the tallow candles flickering in the humid, hot air threw the faces of the President and clerks into bold relief, with curious caricature effects of light and shade.

The petrol lamp above the head of the accused had flared up, and begun to smoke, causing the chimney to crack with a sharp report. This diversion effected a momentary silence among the crowd, and the Public Prosecutor was able to repeat his query:

"Juliette Marny, have you anything to say in reply to the charge brought against you, and why the sentence which I have demanded should not be passed against you?"

The sooty smoke from the lamp came down in small, black, greasy particles; Juliette with her slender finger-tips flicked one of these quietly off her sleeve, then she replied:

"No; I have nothing to say."

"Have you instructed an advocate to defend you, according to your rights of citizenship, which the Law allows?" added the Public Prosecutor solemnly.

Juliette would have replied at once; her mouth had already framed the No with which she meant to answer.

But now at last had come Déroulède's hour. For this he had been silent, had suffered and had held his peace, whilst twice twenty-four hours had dragged their weary lengths along, since the arrest of the woman he loved.

In a moment he was on his feet before them all, accustomed to speak, to dominate, to command.

"Citizeness Juliette Marny has entrusted me with her defence," he said, even before the No had escaped Juliette's white lips, "and I am here to refute the charges brought against her, and to demand in the name of the people of France full acquittal and justice for her."

CHAPTER XXV

THE DEFENCE

Intense excitement, which found vent in loud applause, greeted Déroulède's statement.

"Ça ira! ça ira! vas-y Déroulède! " came from the crowded benches round; and men, women, and children, wearied with the monotony of the past proceedings, settled themselves down for a quarter of an hour's keen enjoyment.

If Déroulède had anything to do with it, the trial was sure to end in excitement. And the people were always ready to listen to their special favourite.

The citizen-deputies, drowsy after the long, oppressive day, seemed to rouse themselves to renewed interest. Lebrun, like a big, shaggy dog, shook himself free from creeping somnolence. Robespierre smiled between his thin lips, and looked across at Merlin to see how the situation affected him. The enmity between the Minister of Justice and Citizen Déroulède was well known, and everyone noted, with added zest, that the former wore a keen look of anticipated triumph.

High up, on one of the topmost benches, sat Citizen Lenoir, the stage-manager of this palpitating drama. He looked down, with obvious satisfaction, at the scene which he himself had suggested last night to the members of the Jacobin Club. Merlin's sharp eyes had tried to pierce the gloom, which wrapped the crowd of spectators, searching vainly to distinguish the broad figure and massive head of the provincial giant.

The light from the petrol lamp shone full on Déroulède's earnest, dark countenance as he looked Juliette's infamous accuser full in the face, but the tallow candles, flickering weirdly on the President's desk, threw Tinville's short, spare figure and large, unkempt head into curious grotesque silhouette.

Juliette apparently had lost none of her calm, and there was no one there sufficiently interested in her personality to note the tinge of delicate colour which, at the first word of Déroulède, had slowly mounted to her pale cheeks.

Tinville waited until the wave of excitement had broken upon the shoals of expectancy.

Then he resumed:

121

"Then, Citizen Déroulède, what have you to say, why sentence should not be passed upon the accused?"

"I have to say that the accused is innocent of every charge brought against her in your indictment," replied Déroulède firmly.

"And how do you substantiate this statement, Citizen-Deputy?" queried Tinville, speaking with mock unctuousness.

"Very simply, Citizen Tinville. The correspondence to which you refer did not belong to the accused, but to me. It consisted of certain communications, which I desired to hold with Marie Antoinette, now a prisoner in the Conciergerie, during my state there as lieutenant-governor. The Citizeness Juliette Marny, by denouncing me, was serving the Republic, for my communications with Marie Antoinette had reference to my own hopes of seeing her quit this country and take refuge in her own native land."

Gradually, as Déroulède spoke, a murmur, like the distant roar of a monstrous breaker, rose among the crowd on the upper benches. As he continued quietly and firmly, so it grew in volume and in intensity, until his last words were drowned in one mighty, thunderous shout of horror and execration.

Déroulède, the friend and idol of the people, the privileged darling of this unruly population, the father of the children, the friend of the women, the sympathiser in all troubles, Papa Déroulède as the little ones called him—he a traitor, self-accused, plotting and planning for an ex-tyrant, a harlot who had called herself a queen, for Marie Antoinette the Austrian, who had desired and worked for the overthrow of France! He, Déroulède, a traitor!

In one moment, as he spoke, the love which in their crude hearts they bore him, that animal primitive love, was turned to sudden, equally irresponsible hate. He had deceived them, laughed at them, tried to bribe them by feeding their little ones!

Bah! the bread of the traitor! It might have choked the children.

Surprise at first had taken their breath away. Already they had marvelled why he should stand up to defend a wanton. And now, probably feeling that he was on the point of being found out, he thought it better to make a clean breast of his own treason, trusting in his popularity, in his power over the people.

Bah!!!

Not one extenuating circumstance did they find in their hardened hearts for him.

He had been their idol, enshrined in their squalid, degraded minds, and now he had fallen, shattered beyond recall, and they hated and loathed him as much as they had loved him before.

And this his enemies noted, and smiled with complete satisfaction.

Merlin heaved a sigh of relief. Tinville nodded his shaggy head, in token of intense delight.

What that provincial coal-heaver had foretold had indeed come to pass.

The populace, that most fickle of all fickle things in this world, had turned all at once against its favourite. This Lenoir had predicted, and the transition had been even more rapid than he had anticipated.

Déroulède had been given a length of rope, and, figuratively speaking, had already hanged himself.

The reality was a mere matter of a few hours now. At dawn to-morrow the guillotine; and the mob of Paris, who yesterday would have torn his detractors limb from limb, would on the morrow be dragging him, with hoots and yells and howls of execration, to the scaffold.

The most shadowy of all footholds, that of the whim of a populace, had already given way under him. His enemies knew it, and were exulting in their triumph. He knew it himself, and stood up, calmly defiant, ready for any event, if only he succeeded in snatching her beautiful head from the ready embrace of the guillotine.

Juliette herself had remained as if entranced. The colour had again fled from her cheeks, leaving them paler, more ashen than before. It seemed as if in this moment she suffered more than human creature could bear, more than any torture she had undergone hitherto.

He would not owe his life to her.

That was the one overwhelming thought in her, which annihilated all others. His love for her was dead, and he would not accept the great sacrifice at her hands.

Thus these two in the supreme moment of their life saw each other, yet did not understand. A word, a touch would have given them both the key to one another's heart, and it now seemed as if death would part them for ever, whilst that great enigma remained unsolved.

The Public Prosecutor had been waiting until the noise had somewhat subsided, and his voice could be heard above the din, then he said, with a smile of ill-concealed satisfaction:

"And is the court, then, to understand, Citizen-Deputy Déroulède, that it was you who tried to burn the treasonable correspondence and to destroy the case which contained it?"

"The treasonable correspondence was mine, and it was I who destroyed it."

"But the accused admitted before Citizen Merlin that she herself was trying to burn certain love letters, that would have brought to light her illicit relationship with another man than yourself," argued Tinville suavely. The rope was perhaps not quite long enough; Déroulède must have all that could be given him, ere this memorable sitting was adjourned.

Déroulède, however, instead of directing his reply straight to his enemy, now turned towards the dense crowd of spectators, on the benches opposite to him.

"Citizens, friends, brothers," he said warmly, "the accused is only a girl, young, innocent knowing nothing of peril or of sin. You all have mothers, sisters, daughters—have you not watched those dear to you in the many moods of which a feminine heart is capable; have you not seen them affectionate, tender, and impulsive? Would you love them so dearly but for the fickleness of their moods? Have you not worshipped them in your hearts, for those sublime impulses which put all man's plans and calculations to shame? Look on the accused, citizens. She loves the Republic, the people of France, and feared that I, an unworthy representative of her sons, was hatching treason against our great mother. That was her first wayward impulse—to stop me before I committed the awful crime, to punish me, or perhaps only to warn me. Does a young girl calculate, citizens? She acts as her heart dictates; her reason but awakes from slumber later on, when the act is done. Then comes repentance sometimes: another impulse of tenderness which we all revere. Would you extract vinegar from rose leaves? Just as readily could you find reason in a young girl's head. Is that a crime? She wished to thwart me in my treason; then, seeing me in peril, the sincere friendship she had for me gained the upper hand once more. She loved my mother, who might be losing a son; she loved my crippled foster-sister; for their sakes, not for mine—a traitor's—did she yield to another, a heavenly impulse, that of saving me from the consequences of my own folly. Was that a crime, citizens? When you are ailing, do not your mothers, sisters, wives tend you? when you are seriously ill, would they not give their heart's blood to save you? and when, in the dark hours of your lives, some deed which you would not openly avow before the world overweights your soul with its burden of remorse, is it not again your womenkind who come to you, with tender words and soothing voices, trying to ease your aching conscience, bringing solace, comfort, and peace? And so it was with the accused, citizens. She had seen my crime, and longed to punish it; she saw those who had befriended her in sorrow, and she tried to ease their pain by taking my guilt upon her shoulders. She has suffered for the noble lie, which she had told on my behalf, as no woman has ever been made to suffer before. She has stood, white and innocent as your new-born children, in the pillory of infamy. She was ready to endure death, and what was ten thousand times worse than death, because of her own warm-hearted affection. But you, citizens of France, who, above all, are noble, true, and chivalrous, you will not allow the sweet impulses of young and tender womanhood to be punished with the ban of felony. To you, women of France, I appeal in the name of your childhood, your girlhood, your motherhood; take her to your hearts, she is worthy of it, worthier now for having blushed before you, worthier than any heroine in the great roll of honour of France."

His magnetic voice went echoing along the rafters of the great, sordid Hall of Justice, filling it with a glory it had never known before. His enthusiasm thrilled his hearers, his appeal to their honour and chivalry roused all the finer feelings within them. Still hating him for his treason, his magical appeal had turned their hearts towards her.

They had listened to him without interruption, and now at last, when he paused, it was very evident, by muttered exclamations and glances cast at Juliette, that popular feeling, which up to the present had practically ignored her, now went out towards her personality with overwhelming sympathy.

Obviously at the present moment, if Juliette's fate had been put to the plebiscite, she would have been unanimously acquitted.

Merlin, as Déroulède spoke, had once or twice tried to read his friend Foucquier-Tinville's enigmatical expression, but the Public Prosecutor, with his face in deep shadow, had not moved a muscle during the Citizen-Deputy's noble peroration. He sat at his desk, chin resting on hand, staring before him with an expression of indifference, almost of boredom.

Now, when Déroulède finished speaking, and the outburst of human enthusiasm had somewhat subsided, he rose slowly to his feet, and said quietly:

"So you maintain, Citizen-Deputy, that the accused is a chaste and innocent girl, unjustly charged with immorality?"

"I do," protested Déroulède loudly.

"And will you tell the court why you are so ready to publicly accuse yourself of treason against the Republic, knowing full well all the consequences of your action?"

"Would any Frenchman care to save his own life at the expense of a woman's honour?" retorted Déroulède proudly.

A murmur of approval greeted these words, and Tinville remarked unctuously:

"Quite so, quite so. We esteem your chivalry, Citizen-Deputy. The same spirit, no doubt, actuates you to maintain that the accused knew nothing of the papers which you say you destroyed?"

"She knew nothing of them. I destroyed them; I did not know that they had been found; on my return to my house I discovered that the Citizeness Juliette Marny had falsely accused herself of having destroyed some papers surreptitiously."

"She said they were love letters."

"It is false."

"You declare her to be pure and chaste?"

"Before the whole world."

"Yet you were in the habit of frequenting the bedroom of this pure and chaste girl, who dwelt under your roof," said Tinville with slow and deliberate sarcasm.

"It is false."

"If it be false, Citizen Déroulède," continued the other with the same unctuous suavity, "then how comes it that the correspondence which you admit was treasonable, and therefore presumably secret—how comes it that it was found, still smouldering, in the chaste young woman's bedroom, and the torn letter-case concealed among her dresses in a valise?"

"It is false."

"The Minister of Justice, Citizen-Deputy Merlin, will answer for the truth of that."

"It is the truth," said Juliette quietly.

Her voice rang out clear, almost triumphant, in the midst of the breathless pause, caused by the previous swift questions and loud answers.

Déroulède now was silent.

This one simple fact he did not know. Anne Mie, in telling him the events in connection with the arrest of Juliette, had omitted to give him the one little detail, that the burnt letters were found in the young girl's bedroom.

Up to the moment when the Public Prosecutor confronted him with it, he had been under the impression that she had destroyed the papers and the letter-case in the study, where she had remained alone after Merlin and his men had left the room. She could easily have burnt them there, as a tiny spirit lamp was always kept alight on a side table for the use of smokers.

This little fact now altered the entire course of events. Tinville had but to frame an indignant ejaculation:

"Citizens of France, see how you are being befooled and hoodwinked!"

Then he turned once more to Déroulède.

"Citizen Déroulède ..." he began.

But in the tumult that ensued he could no longer hear his own voice. The pent-up rage of the entire mob of Paris seemed to find vent for itself in the howls with which the crowd now tried to drown the rest of the proceedings.

As their brutish hearts had been suddenly melted on behalf of Juliette, in response to Déroulède's passionate appeal, so now they swiftly changed their sympathetic attitude to one of horror and execration.

Two people had fooled and deceived them. One of these they had reverenced and trusted, as much as their degraded minds were capable of reverencing anything, therefore his sin seemed doubly damnable.

He and that pale-face aristocrat had for weeks now, months, or years perhaps, conspired against the Republic, against the Revolution, which had been made by a people thirsting for liberty. During these months and years he had talked to them, and they had listened; he had poured forth treasures of eloquence, cajoled them, as he had done just now.

The noise and hubbub were growing apace. If Tinville and Merlin had desired to infuriate the mob, they had more than succeeded. All that was most bestial, most savage in this awful Parisian populace rose to the surface now in one wild, mad desire for revenge.

The crowd rushed down from the benches, over one another's heads, over children's fallen bodies; they rushed down because they wanted to get at him, their whilom favourite, and at his pale-faced mistress, and tear them to pieces, hit them, scratch out their eyes. They snarled like so many wild beasts, the women shrieked, the children cried, and the men of the National Guard, hurrying forward, had much ado to keep back this flood-tide of hate.

Had any of them broken loose, from behind the barrier of bayonets hastily raised against them, it would have fared ill with Déroulède and Juliette.

The President wildly rang his bell, and his voice, quivering with excitement, was heard once or twice above the din.

"Clear the court! Clear the court!"

But the people refused to be cleared out of court.

"A la lanterne les traîtres! Mort à Déroulède. A la lanterne! l'aristo! "

127

And in the thickest of the crowd, the broad shoulders and massive head of Citizen Lenoir towered above the others.

At first it seemed as if he had been urging on the mob in its fury. His strident voice, with its broad provincial accent, was heard distinctly shouting loud vituperations against the accused.

Then at a given moment, when the tumult was at its height, when the National Guard felt their bayonets giving way before this onrushing tide of human jackals, Lenoir changed his tactics.

"Tiens! c'est bête! " he shouted loudly, "we shall do far better with the traitors when we get them outside. What say you, citizens? Shall we leave the judges here to conclude the farce, and arrange for its sequel ourselves outside the 'Tigre Jaune'?"

At first but little heed was paid to his suggestion, and he repeated it once or twice, adding some interesting details:

"One is freer in the streets, where these apes of the National Guard can't get between the people of France and their just revenge. Ma foi! " he added, squaring his broad shoulders, and pushing his way through the crowd towards the door, "I for one am going to see where hangs the most suitable lanterne. "

Like a flock of sheep the crowd now followed him.

"The nearest lanterne! " they shouted. "In the streets—in the streets! A la lanterne! The traitors!"

And with many a jeer, many a loathsome curse, and still more loathsome jests, some of the crowd began to file out. A few only remained to see the conclusion of the farce.

CHAPTER XXVI

SENTENCE OF DEATH

The "Bulletin du Tribunal Révolutionnaire" tells us that both the accused had remained perfectly calm during the turmoil which raged within the bare walls of the Hall of Justice.

Citizen-Deputy Déroulède, however, so the chroniclers aver, though outwardly impassive, was evidently deeply moved. He had very expressive eyes, clear mirrors of the fine, upright soul within, and in them there was a look of intense emotion as he watched the crowd, which he had so often dominated and controlled, now turning in hatred against him.

He seemed actually to be seeing with a spiritual vision, his own popularity wane and die.

But when the thick of the crowd had pushed and jostled itself out of the hall, that transient emotion seemed to disappear, and he allowed himself quietly to be led from the front bench, where he had sat as a privileged member of the National Convention, to a place immediately behind the dock, and between two men of the National Guard.

From that moment he was a prisoner, accused of treason against the Republic, and obviously his mock trial would be hurried through by his triumphant enemies, whilst the temper of the people was at boiling point against him.

Complete silence had succeeded to the raging tumult of the past few moments. Nothing now could be heard in the vast room, save Foucquier-Tinville's hastily whispered instructions to the clerk nearest to him, and the scratch of the latter's quill pen against the paper.

The President was, with equal rapidity, affixing his signature to various papers handed up to him by the other clerks. The few remaining spectators, the deputies, and those among the crowd who had elected to see the close of the debate, were silent and expectant.

Merlin was mopping his forehead as if in intense fatigue after a hard struggle; Robespierre was coolly taking snuff.

From where Déroulède stood, he could see Juliette's graceful figure silhouetted against the light of the petrol lamp. His heart was torn between intense misery at having failed to save her and a curious, exultant joy at thought of dying beside her.

He knew the procedure of this revolutionary tribunal well—

129

knew that within the next few moments he too would be condemned, that they would both be hustled out of the crowd and dragged through the streets of Paris, and finally thrown into the same prison, to herd with those who, like themselves, had but a few hours to live.

And then to-morrow at dawn, death for them both under the guillotine. Death in public, with all its attendant horrors: the packed tumbril; the priest, in civil clothes, appointed by this godless government, muttering conventional prayers and valueless exhortations.

And in his heart there was nothing but love for her—love and an intense pity—for the punishment she was suffering was far greater than her crime. He hoped that in her heart remorse would not be too bitter; and he looked forward with joy to the next few hours, which he would pass near her, during which he could perhaps still console and soothe her.

She was but the victim of an ideal, of Fate stronger than her own will. She stood, an innocent martyr to the great mistake of her life.

But the minutes sped on. Foucquier-Tinville had evidently completed his new indictments.

The one against Juliette Marny was read out first. She was now accused of conspiring with Paul Déroulède against the safety of the Republic, by having cognisance of a treasonable correspondence carried on with the prisoner, Marie Antoinette; by virtue of which accusation the Public Prosecutor asked her if she had anything to say.

"No," she replied loudly and firmly. "I pray to God for the safety and deliverance of our Queen, Marie Antoinette, and for the overthrow of this Reign of Terror and Anarchy."

These words, registered in the "Bulletin du Tribunal Révolutionnaire" were taken as final and irrefutable proofs of her guilt, and she was then summarily condemned to death.

She was then made to step down from the dock and Déroulède to stand in her place.

He listened quietly to the long indictment which Foucquier-Tinville had already framed against him the evening before, in readiness for this contingency. The words "treason against the Republic" occurred conspicuously and repeatedly. The document itself is at one with the thousands of written charges, framed by that odious Foucquier-Tinville during these periods of bloodshed, and which in themselves are the most scathing indictments against the odious travesty of Justice, perpetrated with his help.

Self-accused, and avowedly a traitor, Déroulède was not even asked if he had anything to say; sentence of death was passed on him, with the rapidity and callousness peculiar to these proceedings.

After which Paul Déroulède and Juliette Marny were led forth, under strong escort, into the street.

CHAPTER XXVII

THE FRUCTIDOR RIOTS

Many accounts, more or less authentic, have been published of the events known to history as the "Fructidor Riots."

But this is how it all happened: at any rate it is the version related some few days later in England to the Prince of Wales by no less a personage than Sir Percy Blakeney; and who indeed should know better than The Scarlet Pimpernel himself?

Déroulède and Juliette Marny were the last of the batch of prisoners who were tried on that memorable day of Fructidor.

There had been such a number of these, that all the covered carts in use for the conveyance of prisoners to and from the Hall of Justice had already been despatched with their weighty human load; thus it was that only a rough wooden cart, hoodless and rickety, was available, and into this Déroulède and Juliette were ordered to mount.

It was now close on nine o'clock in the evening. The streets of Paris, sparsely illuminated here and there with solitary oil lamps swung across from house to house on wires, presented a miserable and squalid appearance. A thin, misty rain had begun to fall, transforming the ill-paved roads into morasses of sticky mud.

The Hall of Justice was surrounded by a howling and shrieking mob, who, having imbibed all the stores of brandy in the neighbouring drinking bars, was now waiting outside in the dripping rain for the express purpose of venting its pent-up, spirit-sodden lust of rage against the man whom it had once worshipped, but whom now it hated. Men, women, and even children swarmed round the principal entrances of the Palais de Justice, along the bank of the river as far as the Pont au Change, and up towards the Luxembourg Palace, now transformed into the prison, to which the condemned would no doubt be conveyed.

Along the river-bank, and immediately facing the Palais de Justice, a row of gallows-shaped posts, at intervals of a hundred yards or more, held each a smoky petrol lamp, at a height of some eight feet from the ground.

One of these lamps had been knocked down, and from the post itself there now hung ominously a length of rope, with a noose at the end.

Around this improvised gallows a group of women sat, or

rather squatted, in the mud; their ragged shifts and kirtles, soaked through with the drizzling rain, hung dankly on their emaciated forms; their hair, in some cases grey, and in others dark or straw-coloured, clung matted round their wet faces, on which the dirt and the damp had drawn weird and grotesque lines.

The men were restless and noisy, rushing aimlessly hither and thither, from the corner of the bridge, up the Rue du Palais, fearful lest their prey be conjured away ere their vengeance was satisfied.

Oh, how they hated their former idol now! Citizen Lenoir, with his broad shoulders and powerful, grime-covered head, towered above the throng; his strident voice, with its raucous, provincial accent, could be distinctly heard above the din, egging on the men, shouting to the women, stirring up hatred against the prisoners, wherever it showed signs of abating in intensity.

The coal-heaver, hailing from some distant province, seemed to have set himself the grim task of provoking the infuriated populace to some terrible deed of revenge against Déroulède and Juliette.

The darkness of the street, the fast-falling mist which obscured the light from the meagre oil lamps, seemed to add a certain weirdness to this moving, seething multitude. No one could see his neighbour. In the blackness of the night the muttering or yelling figures moved about like some spectral creatures from hellish regions—the Akous of Brittany who call to those about to die; whilst the women squatting in the oozing mud, beneath that swinging piece of rope, looked like a group of ghostly witches, waiting for the hour of their Sabbath.

As Déroulède emerged into the open, the light from a swinging lantern in the doorway fell upon his face. The foremost of the crowd recognised him; a howl of execration went up to the cloud-covered sky, and a hundred hands were thrust out in deadly menace against him.

It seemed as if they wished to tear him to pieces.

"A la lanterne! A la lanterne! le traître! "

He shivered slightly, as if with the sudden blast of cold, humid air, but he stepped quietly into the cart, closely followed by Juliette.

The strong escort of the National Guard, with Commandant Santerre and his two drummers, had much ado to keep back the mob. It was not the policy of the revolutionary government to allow excesses of summary justice in the streets: the public execution of traitors on the Place de la Révolution, the processions in the tumbrils, were thought to be wholesome examples for other would-be traitors to mark and digest.

Citizen Santerre, military commandant of Paris, had ordered

his men to use their bayonets ruthlessly, and, to further overawe the populace, he ordered a prolonged roll of drums, lest Déroulède took it into his head to speak to the crowd.

But Déroulède had no such intention: he seemed chiefly concerned in shielding Juliette from the cold; she had been made to sit in the cart beside him, and he had taken off his coat, and was wrapping it round her against the penetrating rain.

The eye-witnesses of these memorable events have declared that, at a given moment, he looked up suddenly with a curious, eager expression in his eyes, and then raised himself in the cart and seemed to be trying to penetrate the gloom round him, as if in search of a face, or perhaps a voice.

"A la lanterne! A la lanterne! " was the continual hoarse cry of the mob.

Up to now, flanked in their rear by the outer walls of the Palais de Justice, the soldiers had found it a fairly easy task to keep the crowd at bay. But there came a time when the cart was bound to move out into the open, in order to convey the prisoners along, by the Rue du Palais, up to the Luxembourg Prison.

This task, however, had become more and more difficult every moment. The people of Paris, who for two years had been told by its tyrants that it was supreme lord of the universe, was mad with rage at seeing its desires frustrated by a few soldiers.

The drums had been greeted by terrific yells, which effectually drowned their roll; the first movement of the cart was hailed by a veritable tumult.

Only the women who squatted round the gallows had not moved from their position of vantage; one of these Mægæras was quietly readjusting the rope, which had got out of place.

But all the men and some of the women were literally besieging the cart, and threatening the soldiers, who stood between them and the object of their fury.

It seemed as if nothing now could save Déroulède and Juliette from an immediate and horrible death.

"A mort! A mort! A la lanterne les traîtres! "

Santerne himself, who had shouted himself hoarse, was at a loss what to do. He had sent one man to the nearest cavalry barracks, but reinforcements would still be some little time coming; whilst in the meanwhile his men were getting exhausted, and the mob, more and more excited, threatened to break through their line at every moment.

There was not another second to be lost.

Santerre was for letting the mob have its way, and he would willingly have thrown it the prey for which it clamoured; but orders

134

were orders, and in the year I. of the Revolution it was not good to disobey.

At this supreme moment of perplexity he suddenly felt a respectful touch on his arm.

Close behind him a soldier of the National Guard—not one of his own men—was standing at attention, and holding a small, folded paper in his hand.

"Sent to you by the Minister of Justice," whispered the soldier hurriedly. "The citizen-deputies have watched the tumult from the Hall; they say, you must not lose an instant."

Santerre withdrew from the front rank, up against the side of the cart, where a rough stable lantern had been fixed. He took the paper from the soldier's hand, and, hastily tearing it open, he read it by the dim light of the lantern.

As he read, his thick, coarse features expressed the keenest satisfaction.

"You have two more men with you?" he asked quickly.

"Yes, citizen," replied the man, pointing towards his right; "and the Citizen-Minister said you would give me two more."

"You'll take the prisoners quietly across to the Prison of the Temple —you understand that?"

"Yes, citizen; Citizen Merlin has given me full instructions. You can have the cart drawn back a little more under the shadow of the portico, where the prisoners can be made to alight; they can then be given into my charge. You in the meantime are to stay here with your men, round the empty cart, as long as you can. Reinforcements have been sent for, and must soon be here. When they arrive you are to move along with the cart, as if you were making for the Luxembourg Prison. This manoeuvre will give us time to deliver the prisoners safely at the Temple."

The man spoke hurriedly and peremptorily, and Santerne was only too ready to obey. He felt relieved at thought of reinforcements, and glad to be rid of the responsibility of conducting such troublesome prisoners.

The thick mist, which grew more and more dense, favoured the new manoeuvre, and the constant roll of drums drowned the hastily given orders.

The cart was drawn back into the deepest shadow of the great portico, and whilst the mob were howling their loudest, and yelling out frantic demands for the traitors, Déroulède and Juliette were summarily ordered to step out of the cart. No one saw them, for the darkness here was intense.

"Follow quietly!" whispered a raucous voice in their ears as they did so, "or my orders are to shoot you where you stand."

135

But neither of them had any wish for resistance. Juliette, cold and numb, was clinging to Déroulède, who had placed a protecting arm round her.

Santerne had told off two of his men to join the new escort of the prisoners, and presently the small party, skirting the walls of the Palais de Justice, began to walk rapidly away from the scene of the riot.

Déroulède noted that some half-dozen men seemed to be surrounding him and Juliette, but the drizzling rain blurred every outline. The blackness of the night too had become absolutely dense, and in the distance the cries of the populace grew more and more faint.

CHAPTER XXVIII

THE UNEXPECTED

The small party walked on in silence. It seemed to consist of a very few men of the National Guard, whom Santerne had placed under the command of the soldier who had transmitted to him the orders of the Citizen-Deputies.

Juliette and Déroulède both vaguely wondered whither they were being led; to some other prison mayhap, away from the fury of the populace. They were conscious of a sense of satisfaction at thought of being freed from that pack of raging wild beasts.

Beyond that they cared nothing. Both felt already the shadow of death hovering over them. The supreme moment of their lives had come, and had found them side by side.

What neither fear nor remorse, sorrow nor joy, could do, that the great and mighty Shadow accomplished in a trice.

Juliette, looking death bravely in the face, held out her hand, and sought that of the man she loved.

There was not one word spoken between them, not even a murmur.

Déroulède, with the unerring instinct of his own unselfish passion, understood all that the tiny hand wished to convey to him.

In a moment everything was forgotten save the joy of this touch. Death, or the fear of death, had ceased to exist. Life was beautiful, and in the soul of these two human creatures there was perfect peace, almost perfect happiness.

With one grasp of the hand they had sought and found one another's soul. What mattered the yelling crowd, the noise and tumult of this sordid world? They had found one another, and, hand-in-hand, shoulder-to-shoulder, they had gone off wandering into the land of dreams, where dwelt neither doubt nor treachery, where there was nothing to forgive.

He no longer said: "She does not love me—would she have betrayed me else?" He felt the clinging, trustful touch of her hand, and knew that, with all her faults, her great sin and her lasting sorrow, her woman's heart, Heaven's most priceless treasure, was indeed truly his.

And she knew that he had forgiven—nay, that he had naught to forgive —for Love is sweet and tender, and judges not. Love is

Love—whole, trustful, passionate. Love is perfect understanding and perfect peace.

And so they followed their escort whithersoever it chose to lead them.

Their eyes wandered aimlessly over the mist-laden landscape of this portion of deserted Paris. They had turned away from the river now, and were following the Rue des Arts. Close by on the right was the dismal little hostelry, "La Cruche Cassée," where Sir Percy Blakeney lived. Déroulède, as they neared the place, caught himself vaguely wondering what had become of his English friend.

But it would take more than the ingenuity of the Scarlet Pimpernel to get two noted prisoners out of Paris to-day. Even if ...

"Halt!"

The word of command rang out clearly and distinctly through the rain-soaked atmosphere.

Déroulède threw up his head and listened. Something strange and unaccountable in that same word of command had struck his sensitive ear.

Yet the party had halted, and there was a click as of bayonets or muskets levelled ready to fire.

All had happened in less than a few seconds. The next moment there was a loud cry:

"A moi, Déroulède! 'tis the Scarlet Pimpernel!"

A vigorous blow from an unseen hand had knocked down and extinguished the nearest street lantern.

Déroulède felt that he and Juliette were being hastily dragged under an adjoining doorway even as the cheery voice echoed along the narrow street.

Half-a-dozen men were struggling below in the mud, and there was a plentiful supply of honest English oaths. It looked as if the men of the National Guard had fallen upon one another, and had it not been for those same English oaths perhaps Déroulède and Juliette would have been slower to understand.

"Well done, Tony! Gadzooks, Ffoulkes, that was a smart bit of work!"

The lazy, pleasant voice was unmistakable, but, God in heaven! where did it come from?

Of one thing there could be no doubt. The two men despatched by Santerne were lying disabled on the ground, whilst three other soldiers were busy pinioning them with ropes.

What did it all mean?

"La, friend Déroulède! you had not thought, I trust, that I would leave Mademoiselle Juliette in such a demmed, uncomfortable hole?"

138

And there, close beside Déroulède and Juliette, stood the tall figure of the Jacobin orator, the bloodthirsty Citizen Lenoir. The two young people gazed and gazed, then looked again, dumfounded, hardly daring to trust their vision, for through the grime-covered mask of the gigantic coal-heaver a pair of merry blue eyes was regarding them with lazy-amusement.

"La! I do look a miserable object, I know," said the pseudo coal-heaver at last, "but 'twas the only way to get those murderous devils to do what I wanted. A thousand pardons, mademoiselle; 'twas I brought you to such a terrible pass, but la! you are amongst friends now. Will you deign to forgive me?"

Juliette looked up. Her great, earnest eyes, now swimming in tears, sought those of the brave man who had so nobly stood by her and the man she loved.

"Blakeney ..." began Déroulède.

But Sir Percy quickly interrupted him:

"Hush, man! we have but a few moments. Remember you are in Paris still, and the Lord only knows how we shall all get out of this murderous city to-night. I have said that you and mademoiselle are among friends. That is all for the moment. I had to get you together, or I should have failed. I could only succeed by subjecting you and mademoiselle to terrible indignities. Our League could plan but one rescue, and I had to adopt the best means at my command to have you condemned and led away together. Faith!" he added, with a pleasant laugh, "my friend Tinville will not be pleased when he realises that Citizen Lenoir has dragged the Citizen-Deputies by the nose."

Whilst he spoke he had led Déroulède and Juliette into a dark and narrow room on the ground floor of the hostelry, and presently he called loudly for Brogard, the host of this uninviting abode.

"Brogard!" shouted Sir Percy. "Where is that ass Brogard? La! man," he added as Citizen Brogard, obsequious and fussy, and with pockets stuffed with English gold, came shuffling along, "where do you hide your engaging countenance? Here! another length of rope for the gallant soldiers. Bring them in here, then give them that potion down their throats, as I have prescribed. Demm it! I wish we need not have brought them along, but that devil Santerre might have been suspicious else. They'll come to no harm, though, and can do us no mischief."

He prattled along merrily. Innately kind and chivalrous, he wished to give Déroulède and Juliette time to recover from their dazed surprise.

The transition from dull despair to buoyant hope had been so sudden: it had all happened in less than three minutes.

The scuffle had been short and sudden outside. The two soldiers of Santerne had been taken completely unawares, and the three young lieutenants of the Scarlet Pimpernel had fallen on them with such vigour that they had hardly had time to utter a cry of "Help!"

Moreover, that cry would have been useless. The night was dark and wet, and those citizens who felt ready for excitement were busy mobbing the Hall of Justice, a mile and a half away. One or two heads had appeared at the small windows of the squalid houses opposite, but it was too dark to see anything, and the scuffle had very quickly subsided.

All was silent now in the Rue des Arts, and in the grimy coffee-room of the Cruche Cassée two soldiers of the National Guard were lying bound and gagged, whilst three others were gaily laughing, and wiping their rain-soaked hands and faces.

In the midst of them all stood the tall, athletic figure of the bold adventurer who had planned this impudent coup.

"La! we've got so far, friends, haven't we?" he said cheerily, "and now for the immediate future. We must all be out of Paris to-night, or the guillotine for the lot of us to-morrow."

He spoke gaily, and with that pleasant drawl of his which was so well known in the fashionable assemblies of London; but there was a ring of earnestness in his voice, and his lieutenants looked up at him, ready to obey him in all things, but aware that danger was looming threateningly ahead.

Lord Anthony Dewhurst, Sir Andrew Ffoulkes, and Lord Hastings, dressed as soldiers of the National Guard, had played their part to perfection. Lord Hastings had presented the order to Santerre, and the three young bucks, at the word of command from their chief, had fallen upon and overpowered the two men whom the commandant of Paris had despatched to look after the prisoners.

So far all was well. But how to get out of Paris? Everyone looked to the Scarlet Pimpernel for guidance.

Sir Percy now turned to Juliette, and with the consummate grace which the elaborate etiquette of the times demanded, he made her a courtly bow.

"Mademoiselle de Marny," he said, "allow me to conduct you to a room, which though unworthy of your presence will, nevertheless, enable you to rest quietly for a few minutes, whilst I give my friend Déroulède further advice and instructions. In the room you will find a disguise, which I pray you to don with all haste. La! they are filthy rags, I own, but your life and—and ours depend upon your help."

Gallantly he kissed the tips of her fingers, and opened the door of an adjoining room to enable her to pass through; then he stood aside, so that her final look, as she went, might be for Déroulède.

As soon as the door had closed upon her he once more turned to the men.

"Those uniforms will not do now," he said peremptorily; "there are bundles of abominable clothes here, Tony. Will you all don them as quickly as you can? We must all look as filthy a band of sansculottes to-night as ever walked the streets of Paris."

His lazy drawl had deserted him now. He was the man of action and of thought, the bold adventurer who held the lives of his friends in the hollow of his hand.

The four men hastily obeyed. Lord Anthony Dewhurst—one of the most elegant dandies of London society—had brought forth from a dank cupboard a bundle of clothes, mere rags, filthy but useful.

Within ten minutes the change was accomplished, and four dirty, slouchy figures stood confronting their chief.

"That's capital!" said Sir Percy merrily.

"Now for Mademoiselle de Marny."

Hardly had he spoken when the door of the adjoining room was pushed open, and a horrible apparition stood before the men. A woman in filthy bodice and skirt, with face covered in grime, her yellow hair, matted and greasy, thrust under a dirty and crumpled cap.

A shout of rapturous delight greeted this uncanny apparition.

Juliette, like the true woman she was, had found all her energy and spirits now that she felt that she had an important part to play. She woke from her dream to realise that noble friends had risked their lives for the man she loved and for her.

Of herself she did not think; she only remembered that her presence of mind, her physical and mental strength, would be needed to carry the rescue to a successful end.

Therefore with the rags of a Paris tricotteuse she had also donned her personality. She played her part valiantly, and one look at the perfection of her disguise was sufficient to assure the leader of this band of heroes that his instructions would be carried through to the letter.

Déroulède too now looked the ragged sansculotte to the life, with bare and muddy feet, frayed breeches, and shabby, black-shag spencer. The four men stood waiting together with Juliette, whilst Sir Percy gave them his final instructions.

"We'll mix with the crowd," he said, "and do all that the crowd does. It is for us to see that that unruly crowd does what we want. Mademoiselle de Marny, a thousand congratulations. I entreat you to take hold of my friend Déroulède's hand, and not to let go of it, on any pretext whatever. La! not a difficult task, I ween," he added, with his genial smile; "and yours, Déroulède, is equally easy. I enjoin you to take charge of Mademoiselle Juliette, and on no account to leave her side until we are out of Paris."

"Out of Paris!" echoed Déroulède, with a troubled sigh.

"Aye!" rejoined Sir Percy boldly; "out of Paris! with a howling mob at our heels causing the authorities to take double precautions. And above all remember, friends, that our rallying cry is the shrill call of the sea-mew thrice repeated. Follow it until you are outside the gates of Paris. Once there, listen for it again; it will lead you to freedom and safety at last. Aye! Outside Paris, by the grace of God."

The hearts of his hearers thrilled as they heard him. Who could help but follow this brave and gallant adventurer, with the magic voice and the noble bearing?

"And now en route !" said Blakeney finally, "that ass Santerre will have dispersed the pack of yelling hyenas with his cavalry by now. They'll to the Temple prison to find their prey; we'll in their wake. A moi, friends! and remember the sea-gull's cry."

Déroulède drew Juliette's hand in his.

"We are ready," he said; "and God bless the Scarlet Pimpernel."

Then the five men, with Juliette in their midst, went out into the street once more.

CHAPTER XXIX

PÈRE LACHAISE

It was not difficult to guess which way the crowd had gone; yells, hoots, and hoarse cries could be heard from the farther side of the river.

Citizen Santerne had been unable to keep the mob back until the arrival of the cavalry reinforcements. Within five minutes of the abduction of Déroulède and Juliette the crowd had broken through the line of soldiers, and had stormed the cart, only to find it empty, and the prey disappeared.

"They are safe in the Temple by now!" shouted Santerne hoarsely, in savage triumph at seeing them all baffled.

At first it seemed as if the wrath of the infuriated populace, fooled in its lust for vengeance, would vent itself against the commandant of Paris and his soldiers; for a moment even Santerre's ruddy cheeks had paled at the sudden vision of this unlooked for danger.

Then just as suddenly the cry was raised.

"To the Temple!"

"To the Temple! To the Temple!" came in ready response.

The cry was soon taken up by the entire crowd, and in less than two minutes the purlieus of the Hall of Justice were deserted, and the Pont St Michel, then the Cité and the Pont au Change, swarmed with the rioters. Thence along the north bank of the river, and up the Rue du Temple, the people still yelling, muttering, singing the "Ça ira, " and shouting: "A la lanterne! A la lanterne! "

Sir Percy Blakeney and his little band of followers had found the Pont Neuf and the adjoining streets practically deserted. A few stragglers from the crowd, soaked through with the rain, their enthusiasm damped, and their throats choked with the mist, were sulkily returning to their homes.

The desultory group of six sansculottes attracted little or no attention, and Sir Percy boldly challenged every passer-by.

"The way to the Rue du Temple, citizen?" he asked once or twice, or:

"Have they hung the traitor yet? Can you tell me, citizeness?"

A grunt or an oath were the usual replies, but no one took any further notice of the gigantic coal-heaver and his ragged friends.

At the corner of one of the cross streets, between the Rue du

143

Temple and the Rue des Archives, Sir Percy Blakeney suddenly turned to his followers:

"We are close to the rabble now," he said in a whisper, and speaking in English; "do you all follow the nearest stragglers, and get as soon as possible into the thickest of the crowd. We'll meet again outside the prison—and remember the sea-gull's cry."

He did not wait for an answer, and presently disappeared in the mist.

Already a few stragglers, hangers-on of the multitude, were gradually coming into view, and the yells could be distinctly heard. The mob had evidently assembled in the great square outside the prison, and was loudly demanding the object of its wrath.

The moment for cool-headed action was at hand. The Scarlet Pimpernel had planned the whole thing, but it was for his followers and for those, whom he was endeavouring to rescue from certain death, to help him heart and soul.

Déroulède's grasp tightened on Juliette's little hand.

"Are you frightened, my beloved?" he whispered.

"Not whilst you are near me," she murmured in reply.

A few more minutes' walk up the Rue des Archives and they were in the thick of the crowd. Sir Andrew Ffoulkes, Lord Anthony Dewhurst, and Lord Hastings, the three Englishmen, were in front; Déroulède and Juliette immediately behind them.

The mob itself now carried them along. A motley throng they were, soaked through with the rain, drunk with their own baffled rage, and with the brandy which they had imbibed.

Everyone was shouting; the women louder than the rest; one of them was dragging the length of rope, which might still be useful.

"Ça ira! ça ira! A la lanterne! A la lanterne! les traîtres! "

And Déroulède, holding Juliette by the hand, shouted lustily with them:

"Ça ira! "

Sir Andrew Ffoulkes turned, and laughed. It was rare sport for these young bucks, and they all entered into the spirit of the situation. They all shouted "A la lanterne! " egging and encouraging those around them.

Déroulède and Juliette felt the intoxication of the adventure. They were drunk with the joy of their reunion, and seized with the wild, mad, passionate desire for freedom and for life ... Life and love!

So they pushed and jostled on in the mud, followed the crowd, sang and yelled louder than any of them. Was not that very crowd the great bulwark of their safety?

As well have sought for the proverbial needle in the haystack, as for two escaped prisoners in this mad, heaving throng.

The large open space in front of the Temple Prison looked like one great, seething, black mass.

The darkness was almost thick here, the ground like a morass, with inches of clayey mud, which stuck to everything, whilst the sparse lanterns, hung to the prison walls and beneath the portico, threw practically no light into the square.

As the little band, composed of the three Englishmen, and of Déroulède, holding Juliette by the hand, emerged into the open space, they heard a strident cry, like that of a sea-mew thrice repeated, and a hoarse voice shouting from out the darkness:

"Ma foi! I'll not believe that the prisoners are in the Temple now! It is my belief, friends, citizens, that we have been fooled once more!"

The voice, with its strange, unaccountable accent, which seemed to belong to no province of France, dominated the almost deafening noise; it penetrated through, even into the brandy-soddened minds of the multitude, for the suggestion was received with renewed shouts of the wildest wrath.

Like one great, living, seething mass the crowd literally bore down upon the huge and frowning prison. Pushing, jostling, yelling, the women screaming, the men cursing, it seemed as if that awesome day— the 14th of July—was to have its sanguinary counterpart to-night, as if the Temple were destined to share the fate of the Bastille.

Obedient to their leader's orders the three young Englishmen remained in the thick of the crowd: together with Déroulède they contrived to form a sturdy rampart round Juliette, effectually protecting her against rough buffetings.

On their right, towards the direction of Ménilmontant, the sea-mew's cry at intervals gave the strength and courage.

The foremost rank of the crowd had reached the portico of the building, and, with howls and snatches of their gutter song, were loudly clamouring for the guardian of the grim prison.

No one appeared; the great gates with their massive bars and hinges remained silent and defiant.

The crowd was becoming dangerous: whispers of the victory of the Bastille, five years ago, engendered thoughts of pillage and of arson.

Then the strident voice was heard again:

"Pardi! the prisoners are not in the Temple! The dolts have allowed them to escape, and now are afraid of the wrath of the people!"

It was strange how easily the mob assimilated this new idea. Perhaps the dark, frowning block of massive buildings had overawed them with its peaceful strength, perhaps the dripping rain and oozing clay had damped their desire for an immediate storming of the grim citadel; perhaps it was merely the human characteristic of a wish for something new, something unexpected.

Be that as it may, the cry was certainly taken up with marvellous, quick-change rapidity.

"The prisoners have escaped! The prisoners have escaped!"

Some were for proceeding with the storming of the Temple, but they were in the minority. All along, the crowd had been more inclined for private revenge than for martial deeds of valour; the Bastille had been taken by daylight; the effort might not have been so successful on a pitch-black night such as this, when one could not see one's hand before one's eyes, and the drizzling rain went through to the marrow.

"They've got through one of the barriers by now!" suggested the same voice from out the darkness.

"The barriers—the barriers!" came in sheeplike echo from the crowd.

The little group of fugitives and their friends tightened their hold on one another.

They had understood at last.

"It is for us to see that the crowd does what we want," the Scarlet Pimpernel had said.

He wanted it to take him and his friends out of Paris, and, by God! he was like to succeed.

Juliette's heart within her beat almost to choking; her strong little hand gripped Déroulède's fingers with the wild strength of a mad exultation.

Next to the man to whom she had given her love and her very soul she admired and looked up to the remarkable and noble adventurer, the high-born and exquisite dandy, who with grime-covered face, and strong limbs encased in filthy clothes, was playing the most glorious part ever enacted upon the stage.

"To the barriers—to the barriers!"

Like a herd of wild horses, driven by the whip of the herdsmen, the mob began to scatter in all directions. Not knowing what it wanted, not knowing what it would find, half forgetting the very cause and object of its wrath, it made one gigantic rush for the gates of the great city through which the prisoners were supposed to have escaped.

The three Englishmen and Déroulède, with Juliette well protected in their midst, had not joined the general onrush as yet.

146

The crowd in the open place was still very thick, the outward-branching streets were very narrow: through these the multitude, scampering, hurrying, scurrying, like a human torrent let out of a whirlpool, rushed down headlong towards the barriers.

Up the Rue Turbigo to the Belleville gate, the Rue des Filles, and the Rue du Chemin Vert, towards Popincourt, they ran, knocking each other down, jostling the weaker ones on one side, trampling others underfoot. They were all rough, coarse creatures, accustomed to these wild bousculades, ready to pick themselves up, again after any number of falls; whilst the mud was slimy and soft to tumble on, and those who did the trampling had no shoes on their feet.

They rushed out from the dark, open place, these creatures of the night, into streets darker still.

On they ran—on! on!—now in thick, heaving masses, anon in loose, straggling groups—some north, some south, some east, some west.

But it was from the east that came the seagull's cry.

The little band ran boldly towards the east. Down the Rue de la République they followed their leader's call. The crowd was very thick here; the Barrière Ménilmontant was close by, and beyond it there was the cemetery of Père Lachaise. It was the nearest gate to the Temple Prison, and the mob wanted to be up and doing, not to spend too much time running along the muddy streets and getting wet and cold, but to repeat the glorious exploits of the 14th of July, and capture the barriers of Paris by force of will rather than force of arms.

In this rushing mob the four men, with Juliette in their midst, remained quite unchallenged, mere units in an unruly crowd.

In a quarter of an hour Ménilmontant was reached.

The great gates of the city were well guarded by detachments of the National Guard, each under command of an officer. Twenty strong at most—what was that against such a throng?

Who had ever dreamed of Paris being stormed from within?

At every gate to the north and east of the city there was now a rabble some four or five thousand strong, wanting it knew not what. Everyone had forgotten what it was that caused him or her to rush on so blindly, so madly, towards the nearest barrier.

But everyone knew that he or she wanted to get through that barrier, to attack the soldiery, to knock down the captain of the Guard.

And with a wild cry every city gate was stormed.

Like one huge wind-tossed wave, the populace on that memorable night of Fructidor, broke against the cordon of soldiery, that vainly tried to keep it back. Men and women, drunk with brandy and exultation, shouted "Quatorze Juillet! " and amidst curses and threats demanded the opening of the gates.

The people of France would have its will.

Was it not the supreme lord and ruler of the land, the arbiter of the Fate of this great, beautiful, and maddened country?

The National Guard was powerless; the officers in command could offer but feeble resistance.

The desultory fire, which in the darkness and the pouring rain did very little harm, had the effect of further infuriating the mob.

The drizzle had turned to a deluge, a veritable heavy summer downpour, with occasional distant claps of thunder and incessant sheet-lightning, which ever and anon illumined with its weird, fantastic flash this heaving throng, these begrimed faces, crowned with red caps of Liberty, these witchlike female creatures with wet, straggly hair and gaunt, menacing arms.

Within half-an-hour the people of Paris was outside its own gates.

Victory was complete. The Guard did not resist; the officers had surrendered; the great and mighty rabble had had its way.

Exultant, it swarmed around the fortifications and along the terrains vagues which it had conquered by its will.

But the downpour was continuous, and with victory came satiety— satiety coupled with wet skins, muddy feet, tired, wearied bodies, and throats parched with continual shouting.

At Ménilmontant, where the crowd had been thickest, the tempers highest, and the yells most strident, there now stretched before this tired, excited throng, the peaceful vastness of the cemetery of Père Lachaise.

The great alleys of sombre monuments, the weird cedars with their fantastic branches, like arms of a hundred ghosts, quelled and awed these hooting masses of degraded humanity.

The silent majesty of this city of the dead seemed to frown with withering scorn on the passions of the sister city.

Instinctively the rabble was cowed. The cemetery looked dark, dismal, and deserted. The flashes of lightning seemed to reveal ghostlike processions of the departed heroes of France, wandering silently amidst the tombs.

And the populace turned with a shudder away from this vast place of eternal peace.

From within the cemetery gates, there was suddenly heard the sound of a sea-mew calling thrice to its mate. And five dark figures, wrapped in cloaks, gradually detached themselves from the throng, and one by one slipped into the grounds of Père Lachaise through that break in the wall, which is quite close to the main entrance.

Once more the sea-gull's cry.

Those in the crowd who heard it, shivered beneath their dripping clothes. They thought it was a soul in pain risen from one of the graves, and some of the women, forgetting the last few years of godlessness, hastily crossed themselves, and muttered an invocation to the Virgin Mary.

Within the gates all was silent and at peace. The sodden earth gave forth no echo of the muffled footsteps, which slowly crept towards the massive block of stone, which covers the graves of the immortal lovers —Abélard and Heloïse.

CHAPTER XXX

CONCLUSION

There is but little else to record.

History has told us how, shamefaced, tired, dripping, the great, all-powerful people of Paris quietly slunk back to their homes, even before the first cock-crow in the villages beyond the gates, acclaimed the pale streak of dawn.

But long before that, even before the church bells of the great city had tolled the midnight hour, Sir Percy Blakeney and his little band of followers had reached the little tavern which stands close to the farthest gate of Père Lachaise.

Without a word, like six silent ghosts, they had traversed the vast cemetery, and reached the quiet hostelry, where the sounds of the seething revolution only came, attenuated by their passage through the peaceful city of the dead.

English gold had easily purchased silence and good will from the half-starved keeper of this wayside inn. A huge travelling chaise already stood in readiness, and four good Flanders horses had been pawing the ground impatiently for the past half hour. From the window of the chaise old Pétronelle's face, wet with anxious tears, was peering anxiously.

A cry of joy and surprise escaped Déroulède and Juliette, and both turned, with a feeling akin to awe, towards the wonderful man who had planned and carried through this bold adventure.

"Nay, my friend," said Sir Percy, speaking more especially to Déroulède; "if you only knew how simple it all was! Gold can do so many things, and my only merit seems to be the possession of plenty of that commodity. You told me yourself how you had provided for old Pétronelle. Under the most solemn assurance that she would meet her young mistress here, I got her to leave Paris. She came out most bravely this morning in one of the market carts. She is so obviously a woman of the people, that no one suspected her. As for the worthy couple who keep this wayside hostel, they have been well paid, and money soon procures a chaise and horses. My English friends and I, we have our own passports, and one for Mademoiselle Juliette, who must travel as an English lady, with her old nurse, Pétronelle. There are some decent clothes in readiness for us all in the inn. A quarter of an hour in which to don them and we must on our way. You can use your own passport, of course; your arrest has been so very sudden that it has not yet been cancelled, and we have an eight hours' start of our enemies. They'll wake up to-morrow morning, begad! and find that you have slipped through their fingers."

He spoke with easy carelessness, and that slow drawl of his, as if he were talking airy nothings in a London drawing-room, instead of recounting the most daring, most colossal piece of effrontery the adventurous brain of man could conceive.

Déroulède could say nothing. His own noble heart was too full of gratitude towards his friend to express it all in a few words.

And time, of course, was precious.

Within the prescribed quarter of an hour the little band of heroes had doffed their grimy, ragged clothes, and now appeared dressed as respectable bourgeois of Paris en route for the country. Sir Percy Blakeney had donned the livery of a coachman of a well-to-do house, whilst Lord Anthony Dewhurst wore that of an English lacquey.

Five minutes later Déroulède had lifted Juliette into the travelling chaise, and in spite of fatigue, of anxiety, and emotion, it was immeasurable happiness to feel her arm encircling his shoulders in perfect joy and trust.

Sir Andrew Ffoulkes and Lord Hastings joined them inside the chaise; Lord Anthony sat next to Sir Percy on the box.

And whilst the crowd of Paris was still wondering why it had stormed the gates of the city, the escaped prisoners were borne along the muddy roads of France at breakneck speed northward to the coast.

Sir Percy Blakeney held the reins himself. With his noble heart full of joy, the gallant adventurer himself drove his friends to safety.

They had an eight hours' start, and The League of The Scarlet Pimpernel had done its work thoroughly: well provided with passports, and with relays awaiting them at every station of fifty miles or so, the journey, though wearisome was free from further adventure.

At Le Havre the little party embarked on board Sir Percy Blakeney's yacht the Daydream, where they met Madame Déroulède and Anne Mie.

The two ladies, acting under the instructions of Sir Percy, had as originally arranged, pursued their journey northwards, to the populous seaport town.

Anne Mie's first meeting with Juliette was intensely pathetic. The poor little cripple had spent the last few days in an agony of remorse, whilst the heavy travelling chaise bore her farther and farther away from Paris.

She thought Juliette dead, and Paul a prey to despair, and her tender soul ached when she remembered that it was she who had given the final deadly stab to the heart of the man she loved.

Hers was the nature born to abnegation: aye! and one destined to find bliss therein. And when one glance in Paul Déroulède's face told her that she was forgiven, her cup of joy at seeing him happy beside his beloved, was unalloyed with any bitterness.

It was in the beautiful, rosy dawn of one of the last days of that memorable Fructidor, when Juliette and Paul Déroulède, standing on the deck of the Daydream, saw the shores of France gradually receding from their view.

Déroulède's arm was round his beloved, her golden hair, fanned by the breeze, brushed lightly against his cheek.

"Madonna!" he murmured.

She turned her head to him. It was the first time that they were quite alone, the first time that all thought of danger had become a mere dream.

What had the future in store for them, in that beautiful, strange land to which the graceful yacht was swiftly bearing them?

England, the land of freedom, would shelter their happiness and their joy; and they looked out towards the North, where lay, still hidden in the arms of the distant horizon, the white cliffs of Albion, whilst the mist even now was wrapping in its obliterating embrace the shores of the land where they had both suffered, where they had both learned to love.

He took her in his arms.

"My wife!" he whispered.

The rosy light touched her golden hair; he raised her face to his, and soul met soul in one long, passionate kiss.